DEADLY ENCOUNTER!

Bodie had just enough time to register the roar of an engine, before a car erupted out of nowhere, heading straight for him. His leap was sheer instinct. It took him out of range of the front wheel by no more than a millimetre. He hit the ground, rolling, as the driver swerved towards Kodai and dropped speed. Doyle's shot whanged off the front mudguard, as Kodai wrenched open the passenger door and flung himself across the seat. With the door still flapping wildly, the car slewed away and screamed out of sight . . .

Also by Ken Blake in Sphere Books:

THE PROFESSIONALS 1: WHERE THE JUNGLE ENDS
THE PROFESSIONALS 2: LONG SHOT
THE PROFESSIONALS 3: STAKE OUT
THE PROFESSIONALS 4: HUNTER HUNTED
THE PROFESSIONALS 5: BLIND RUN
THE PROFESSIONALS 6: FALL GIRL

THE PROFESSIONALS:
Hiding to Nothing

KEN BLAKE

Based on the original screenplays by **Ted Childs, John Goldsmith and Michael Feeny Callan**

SPHERE BOOKS LIMITED
30/32 Gray's Inn Road, London WC1X 8JL

First published by Sphere Books Ltd 1980

Set in Intertype Baskerville

Printed in Great Britain by
William Collins Sons & Co Ltd
Glasgow

Chapter One

The London Docks had about them the look of an under-developed photograph. Slate-grey clouds let through a dull, pearly light that smudged the definition between concrete buildings, grimy warehouses, the quay-side and the dark, looming hulls of ships. Only one dash of colour relieved the leadenness of it all – the bright yellow of a crane's jib, like a brilliant swipe of an artist's brush on a blank canvas, as it swung a packing case away from a moored ship.

For a moment, it seemed that the crane was the only thing moving in the entire static scene. Then three men appeared, walking down the ship's gangway. Two of them were as unexceptional in their appearance as the background they moved against: one wore the uniform of a Customs Official, the other that of a ship's Captain. The man walking between them, though, would have attracted attention under any circumstances. In his late thirties, prematurely grey, he was clothed in the black rags of what had once been a Chinese-style tunic: the sort of makeshift uniform that anyone who had watched newscasts of the fighting in Vietnam would recognise at once.

His clothes, together with a sombre, heavily scarred face and cropped hair, gave him a sinister appearance; but more than any of these things, it was the look in his eyes that marked him out as different: different from those who live safe, ordinary lives; different from those whose greatest worries are about the mortgage, or promotion chances, or whether the 7.10 will be late again. His eyes were those of a man who had seen Hell – seen it, lived in it, suffered it.

That haunted stare would never entirely soften. It would be there when he faced himself in the shaving-mirror; during the most ordinary, commonplace moment, people would see it and shudder. It lay behind his gaze as he scanned the quayside, searching for something as the other two men escorted him to an office some fifty yards from the ship.

Just before they reached the office door, he spotted a workman unloading cans of fuel from a flatbed truck and stacking them next to the door of a fuel store. Without breaking his stride, and without appearing unduly interested, he took the scene in. Then he allowed himself to be ushered into the office.

The room was as colourless and as functional as the dockside itself. A couple of ancient desks, a steel filing cabinet, a few wooden chairs. The man sat stiffly in one of the straight-backed chairs, as the Customs Official and the Captain conferred. He stared straight ahead. A second Customs man got up from his desk and walked over, smiling to put the captive at his ease.

'Cup o' tea?' he asked.

There was no response, so he tried again.

'Coffee?'

The man neither spoke, nor looked at him.

Go to Hell, then, thought the Customs man and walked away to where his superior was talking to the ship's Captain.

'So you think he got aboard at Amsterdam?' Dale, as senior Customs Official, needed to get the story straight for his report. Stowaways weren't that unusual – just part of a routine week's work – but each incident had to be meticulously logged and reported on. Most often, the freeloader would have simply been short of cash for his ticket; but every now and then, there was a more sinister reason.

The Captain struggled with his English: 'Ja, ja ... in the hold we find him hiding ...'

Something outside the window caught Dale's eye and he cut the man short. 'Just a minute, Captain ...' Dale moved closer to the window. A car, driven by a Port of

London Authority policeman, drew up and the uniformed officer climbed out. Dale went outside to meet him.

'We've got a stowaway,' he moved back into the office with the policeman, adding ironically, 'talkative bloke.' The prisoner looked up at them briefly, but seemed to show no interest in the new arrival. He fumbled in a pocket for a moment, produced a crumpled packet of cigarettes, and turned towards the man who had made the offer of tea.

'Got a light?' he growled.

Neither his tone, nor the accompanying look, made many concessions to friendship. Even so, the officer moved over, smiling, and proffering his lighter. There was a moment's pause as he thumbed the wheel and angled the flame.

The sudden explosion of violence, when it came, numbed the officer's brain. In one brutally fluent motion, the prisoner grabbed his hand, snatched the lighter, yanked him off balance and hurled him across the room. Before anyone had a chance to react, the fugitive had made it to the door, overturned a chair to hinder pursuit, and then was sprinting down the quay towards the store where the workman was still unloading petrol cans.

He had only a second to look up from his work, before a flexed hand chopped into the side of his neck and his attacker, grabbing two cans of petrol, crashed into the store. Dale and the policeman were thirty yards back: taken completely by surprise. By the time they reached the scene, the stowaway had broken open one of the cans and was sloshing petrol around crazily, splashing it on the walls, the floor, the other neatly piled fuel containers. As they burst in the door, the man was facing them, his face set and determined, the lighter clutched in an outstretched hand. Just below that hand was one of the cans, overturned, petrol still gouting from its lip. The thin, noxious smell of the fuel was all but overpowering in the confined space.

For the space of two heartbeats, no one moved. Then the hand holding the lighter flexed and came closer to the spilled petrol. The watchers flinched, then tensed; they knew that none of them stood the chance of a snowball in Hell if a naked flame hit so much fuel. The man paused again: and when he spoke his voice was taut as a barbed-wire strand.

'Cowley,' he snapped. 'George Cowley. CI5. Get him here. Tell him it's Meredith ... and *get him here* ...' again he thrust the lighter towards the pool of petrol, '... *fast!*'

George Cowley, Head of CI5, stopped in the church porch to settle his black bowler hat on his head, and peered up at the lowering sky. The right weather for a memorial service, he thought. Fitting. Cowley had seen many deaths – violent deaths – in his time. From Military Intelligence he'd gone to MI5 and now to the recently formed CI5, a department made up of hand-picked operatives who were as tough, and as lethal, as the assignments they tackled. Cowley knew that death never waited on circumstance. For him and his men, the risk of a violent end was always present; that fact gave them their edge: kept their nerves strung tight, their reflexes needle-sharp. But when it came to the last rites, Cowley was a traditionalist; he liked things to be done with a proper, sombre respect.

He was joined in the porch by a small group of men, bowler-hatted, like himself, and wearing dark topcoats. One of them, Sir Peter Pelham, led Cowley away from the rest of the group as they made their way through the churchyard.

They walked in silence for a short while. Then, as if he'd been reading his companion's mind, Cowley said: 'He was one of the best men we've ever had, Sir Peter.' Pelham seemed to think on the notion for a second.

'A strange ending for him,' he replied finally. Both men had come to a halt beside a fresh grave and were staring down at it. The even mound of damp, dark soil was littered with a few flints and the occasional stark white root. No headstone was there, nothing to give a name or history to the person who lay beneath, nothing to show that anyone cared or remembered.

'Anonymity was what he sought all his life,' murmured Cowley, without looking up. 'It was his stock-in-trade.' He gestured towards the bare earth. 'And what could be more anonymous than that?' He was lost in thought for a moment; then both men continued on their way towards the church gate.

'When I go,' observed Sir Peter, 'I suppose it'll be an obituary in *The Times* and a pompous memorial service at some fashionable church. Yet he –' Sir Peter glanced back at the grave, '– did more for his country than I could ever hope to do.'

'You're too modest, Sir Peter.' Cowley glanced across and caught the other's wry smile.

'That's just what I'm not, Cowley. I have single-mindedly pursued public recognition. To be quite frank, I can't think of anything I'd enjoy more than reading my own obituary.'

Cowley smiled in turn. He knew full-well that Sir Peter Pelham possessed the somewhat over-developed ego of the career-diplomat. He risked a joke:

'On the grounds that even the press doesn't speak ill of the dead?'

Sir Peter's smile broadened. 'Precisely. And what about you, Cowley? What will it be for you? A marble monument or an unmarked grave?'

They both knew the answer to the question – just as they both knew that if one of them was to die a sudden, violent death, it wouldn't be the urbane diplomat whose calm, ordered existence rarely caused him to be faced with anything more dangerous than briskly revolving doors or a golf ball in flight.

Cowley steered away from the subject. 'It's not a subject I think about a great deal, Sir Peter.'

'If I had your job, I'd think about it most of the time,' came the response; and as if on-cue, the bleeper in Cowley's breast pocket began a high-pitched *blip-blip-blip*.

Pelham appreciated the timing and raised an eyebrow.

'No peace for CI5,' he observed.

Cowley was brusque now. 'Not even here. If you'll excuse me ...'

They shook hands hurriedly and Cowley quickened his pace, heading for his car which was parked just outside the churchyard. Yanking the door open, he snatched the R/T under the dashboard and listened with impatience while he was given a fast run-down on what had happened at the docks. The engine was running and the car in gear before the message was complete. He responded with one sentence: 'I'll be there in half an hour,' then let the clutch in and roared away from the church gate.

Cowley hadn't been the only person contacted by CI5 control. No one knew what Meredith wanted; no one, as yet, had any idea of his motive – or who he was. But the message had come through, loud and clear, that a man was standing knee-deep in petrol, inside a fuel store, waving a cigarette lighter and demanding to see A-squad's head man – and that certainly called for a back-up team. It would come as no surprise to George Cowley to discover Bodie and Doyle already at the docks when he arrived.

When Cowley had been given the job of forming a new squad to fight organised and violent crime, he'd known that the men he picked would have to be special – very special. They'd be going up against killers, fanatics – men without pity and without fear, whether they were motivated by greed, or the lust for power; whether their cause was political, or whether they were hired guns, with no allegiance except to themselves. Crime,

Cowley knew, had lost its amateur status. The opposition nowadays was highly trained, ruthless and had little to lose.

He needed hard men: an elite; and he'd selected them after the most thorough screening, the most rigorous tests. It said a lot for their qualities that Bodie and Doyle had been among the first chosen – and in the shortest time!

As their car screeched into the dock area, both men were tensed for action. Doyle's door was open almost before Bodie had brought the car to a stop some forty yards from the fuel store. As they scanned the area in their usual alert way, they could hear Dale's voice, blurred slightly by a loud-hailer.

'Meredith!' The amplified boom sounded harsh in the artificial silence. 'Meredith! Cowley's on his way. Why not come out? What's the point of all this?' Nothing moved inside the fuel store.

'Can you hear me?' Dale persisted 'Meredith? Give yourself up!'

Still no response, though everyone was looking towards the shed. Then heads turned for a second, as Cowley's car drew up. Bodie and Doyle walked over as their chief climbed out of the driving seat. As they approached the store, Bodie offered a curt piece of information: 'They've managed to keep the press away.'

'Good!' Cowley had no words to waste.

Doyle it was who asked the obvious question: 'Who is this Meredith character?'

As they approached Dale, but before they were within earshot, Cowley provided the answer. 'An old friend from the Hong Kong station – and one of the best men I ever had.' He hesitated a second, then added, 'Until half an hour ago, I thought he was dead.' He waved an ID at Dale and nodded towards the shed.

'In there?'

'Yes, sir.'

'Just leave this to me,' – this last remark directed at

Bodie and Doyle. Then Cowley started to walk towards the shed.

Inside, Meredith caught the merest sound from beyond the door and his hand tightened on the lighter. He watched, ready for anything, as the door opened and a figure was silhouetted against the light. Without pausing in his stride, without taking his eyes from the other man's face, Cowley walked across the shed and took the lighter from Meredith's hand.

Neither man moved; then Meredith said, 'Cowley,' half in greeting, half in affirmation, and the moment of tension was broken. When he spoke, Cowley's voice was deliberately casual.

'I'm glad to see you alive, Colin. The report said "Captured – assume dead".'

Meredith's laugh was harsh. 'It was a fair assumption.'

'Come on,' said Cowley softly, 'let's get you out of this.'

As they left the store, Dale started forward, but Cowley flashed him a look. 'We'll take care of the formalities.' Dale wasn't about to argue with CI5; but before he could get a word out, his attention was taken by Meredith. The man was ashen, swaying on his feet; then his knees buckled and Doyle stepped quickly in to support him as his eyes rolled upwards and he began to drop. Carefully, Doyle lowered Meredith's torso on to the ground as Cowley bent over him.

'Just exhaustion, I think.' Cowley glanced up at Dale. 'Is there anywhere he can rest?'

'There's the office.'

As Bodie and Doyle supported the half-conscious man, Cowley turned to Dale and the policeman.

'What's happened here today ... didn't happen.' He looked from one man to the other. 'Is that understood?' It wasn't a question – and they knew it.

Inside the office, Meredith took the glass of water proffered by Doyle and sipped at it shakily.

'Thanks. But I could do with something stronger.' Bodie looked around. 'The only spirit they've got is surgical,' he observed and shrugged apologetically.

'Feeling better?' – this from Cowley as he joined them.

Meredith nodded. 'Sorry about that, George. But three days ago I was still a guest of the Khmer Rouge and I haven't stopped moving since I got out.'

None of the three men commented: they took the statement as an explanation rather than as an apology. They'd all been in tight spots themselves more times than they cared to remember. The exhausted reaction to danger, to being on the run – even to fear – was well understood.

It was down to Cowley to ask the leading question: 'That was one hell of an arrival you staged. Why the big production number?'

Meredith managed a weak grin. 'It got you here in half an hour.'

'We are on the phone, you know,' Bodie chipped in.

Meredith looked up at him and this time there was an edge to his voice. 'And I'm a stowaway – no name, no papers, no official identity; just a story no *official* mind is ever likely to grasp.'

This gave Cowley his lead. 'Well, let's have the story, Colin. Starting with how you got out of Cambodia.'

Meredith stood up and paced the room for a minute. Then, with what seemed a perfect sense of timing, he turned to face Cowley and said, 'Radouk got me out.' It was uttered flatly, without any attempt at dramatic effect, but Cowley's reaction to the name was immediate.

'Radouk? But he's KGB.'

'Was,' Meredith corrected him. 'Then China's top man – again in the past tense. And right now, he wants to negotiate a new deal – with you.'

'What sort of a deal?' Cowley's tone of voice betrayed a mixture of excitement and wariness. A top agent from the other side was always valuable to British Intelligence.

Sometimes more than just valuable – the information such a man could give might well change the balance of power in the deadly, undercover war that Cowley and his men waged; a war that rarely afforded the chance for glory or decisive victories, but which brought death just as surely as any battlefield. Cowley's war had no truck with medals, troop movements or patriotic headlines. It took place in a twilight world of espionage, secrecy and deadly double-guessing. *What sort of a deal* ... It was always a trade-off of some sort in cases like these. The trick was to make sure you came out with the best of the bargain.

Meredith gave Cowley the answer he'd hoped for. 'Radouk wants a new identity and a lot of money. And he wants them fast. Or he's dead ... and he knows it.'

'What do we get?' Cowley was impatient to know.

'You get a name. The name of a traitor, a double-agent at the very top of Western Intelligence.'

As a bargain, it was second to none. The name of a 'mole' – the most dangerous factor in the twilight war, the enemy within, who could destroy the best-laid strategies almost before they'd been used, could use his influence and power to affect vital events, or send valuable and brave men to their deaths.

Cowley considered for a moment. When he spoke, his voice was deceptively quiet. 'Where do you fit into all this, Colin?'

'I'm his go-between. That's why he got me out of Cambodia.' Meredith hesitated and looked at Cowley levelly. 'And that's why Moscow have sent Igor Kodai after me.'

A second name; a second shock. *'Kodai?'* There was something more than surprise in Cowley's uttering of the name; something bitter. 'They're really giving you star treatment.'

'Nothing but the best. He nearly got me in Amsterdam; it won't take him long to find me here.'

'About as long as it takes to read a shipping schedule,'

Cowley snapped. 'Come on,' he added urgently, 'we're getting you out of here.'

Bodie and Doyle hadn't been slow to detect that note of urgency. As they crossed the quayside, flanking Meredith and their chief, their eyes were quartering the dock, looking for likely hiding places, for anything that would provide cover. They were still twenty yards from the cars, when they heard the sharp *crack* of a high-powered rifle and saw Meredith suddenly spin and fall, the impact of the bullet yanking him forward. They moved instantly, their adrenalin already high, their actions fast and economical.

Before the echo of the shot had faded, they'd lifted Meredith, sheltering his body and dragging him to the nearest car. Cowley ducked low, weaving as he ran. A second shot rang out, the bullet passing him so close that he could hear its lethal whine.

He gained cover as Bodie, his own gun drawn, inched forward to try to pinpoint the assassin's position. Doyle was attending to Meredith, ignoring the continuing fire from the rifle. Cowley edged closer and looked at Doyle questioningly.

'He'll live!' There was blood – a lot of it – but the bullet had taken Meredith in the fleshy part of the forearm. The shock wasn't going to help a man in his weakened condition, but it wouldn't finish him.

Satisfied, Cowley turned away as Bodie snapped off a couple of shots. He'd got a fix on the gunman's vantage point high above them and was close enough with his return fire to make it an uncomfortable place to be. Their attacker's silhouette came into view, then found fresh cover before Bodie could get him in the sights.

Cowley heaved the wounded man off the ground and bundled him into a car.

'I'll see to Meredith,' he said.

The partners took the hint. Guns drawn, they moved out from behind the car, bent low and running hard.

Since the gunman had broken cover, there had been no more shots and they knew that he must be looking for a way out. He'd missed his chance; now his task was to survive and complete his assignment at some other time ... in some other place. Bodie and Doyle knew that next time he'd have more time to pick his killing ground. They had to nail the assassin *now*.

They ran in a fast zig-zag, trying to guess the gunman's route. Some disused warehouse buildings afforded a quick breathing space and a moment for decision. Then the pair moved again, more cautiously this time, down an alleyway between the high, grimy warehouse walls, until they reached the corner of the building. Doyle raised his gun and then moved forward a fraction of an inch, offering no more than an eye and a hank of tousled hair as a target.

A bullet slammed into the brickwork just above his head, then sang off into space. He whipped back, looked across the alley to where Bodie stood, holding his gun low and with both hands, ready for what would come next. Bodie nodded. No more was needed. They'd been through this enough times for it to be almost second-nature.

As Doyle swung into the open, loosing off shots, Bodie moved with the speed of a striking snake: crossing the intersection, hitting the far wall, and bringing his weapon up to provide a cross-fire. But there were no answering shots. The partners waited a second, to be sure, then stepped into the open. Still nothing. They exchanged a glance, then Doyle sprinted to the end of the alley. Kodai was sixty yards ahead and going like hell. Doyle managed to loose off one round – missing – before his quarry ducked out of sight into a doorway.

Kodai knew his trade; though it's likely that he would have thought of it not as a trade but a craft, this business of killing people. Nerveless, his senses honed to a fine edge, he was an expert on murder in the same way that other men might specialise in fine china or antique furniture. He knew his weapons; he knew the methods for killing; he knew how to choose his terrain and get the best from it. Most importantly, he knew how to out-guess an opponent. Or thought he did.

As things stood, Kodai had found cover, Doyle was out in no-man's land. The next move would be for Doyle to get out of sight too; then the cat and mouse game would begin. Most people would have played it that way. Kodai would have played it that way. He hadn't counted on Doyle's ability to out-bluff a bluffer.

He peered round the doorway to find Doyle almost on him. The surprise would have held most men for a crucial, deadly second. Not Kodai. He hurled himself back into the doorway and had disappeared into the building as Doyle's shot zipped past harmlessly. Bodie appeared on the scene almost instantly. Their ploy had worked perfectly – except that the prey had escaped.

The look that passed between them clearly said: *This guy's a pro.* Then Doyle turned and sprinted off towards the back of the building as Bodie sidled up to the door, gathered himself, then slammed through, moving quickly out of the light and traversing the room with his gun-muzzle. The door clattered on its hinges; then there was utter silence. The rooms and corridors seemed deserted. Bodie moved softly along the corridor directly ahead, his ears straining to pick up the least sound. Soon, things would become complicated by the fact that Doyle was moving in from the other side. A footfall or the click of a door could as well be his partner as Kodai.

A flight of stairs lay ahead and Bodie took them two at a time, stepping always on the outside of the treads to lessen the possibility of creakings. As he reached a turn on the stairs, he slowed cautiously. A bullet whirred past his face and ploughed into the wall behind him.

On the ground floor, Doyle heard the shot and raced towards a stairway on his side of the building. Above him, he could hear pounding footsteps – Bodie's, as he lit after the retreating figure of Kodai, throwing caution to the winds and covering the length of the first-floor corridor in one headlong dash to arrive at the solitary door – the only route his quarry could have taken. He paused to listen, stepped back, took the lock out with one massive flat-footed kick and exploded into the room.

Almost before he'd had time to recover his balance, a door on the opposite side of the room cannoned back: an exact replica of his own movement brought Doyle in to face him. For a moment out of time, their guns were trained on each other, their fingers tight on light-action triggers, their nerve-endings raw with tension. In that moment, most men would have killed – shock and an instinct for self-preservation would have pulled the trigger for them. Bodie and Doyle lowered their weapons and looked up, simultaneously, to the open skylight which had been Kodai's exit from the room. That was the thing about Cowley's operatives – they *were* very special.

Again, the partners split up: Doyle turning to race back the way he had come, while Bodie took the steel ladder leading to the skylight. He poked his head out, to see Kodai running across the flat roof of the building. Back outside, Doyle looked up and caught a glimpse of the two figures, hunter and hunted, then lost them as they went behind a bristling forest of chimney stacks.

Kodai hadn't expected to get that lucky! Summoning extra speed from his tiring legs, he managed to lose Bodie for just long enough to get out of sight behind a chimney. As his pursuer came abreast of him, Kodai swung his rifle like a club, catching Bodie just under the rib cage and dropping him instantly. The gun flew from his grip, but Kodai wasn't hanging around to collect it. Leaving the cluster of chimneys, he pounded across the open space of the roof – and in that second Doyle saw him and fired.

He shot wide; but it was enough to send Kodai to ground again. Yanking a pistol from its shoulder holster, he pumped a couple of rounds in Doyle's general direction, coming close, giving himself enough time to get to the top of a nearby fire-escape.

The blow that Bodie had taken to the solar-plexus would have stopped an ox in its tracks: despite which, his foot hit the top rung of the fire-escape as Kodai reached the ground. Even so, the fleeing figure was far ahead of him, moving fast across the quayside, then swerving out of sight by a building near the dock wall. Ahead of him was a tall, wire-mesh gate, firmly padlocked. Kodai fired twice at the lock, yanked at the smashed links, hauled the gate open and was into the street, his legs pumping, his lungs grabbing at air. Away clear ... until he saw, ahead of him, the figure of Bodie atop the high, dockside wall.

'It's always an advantage,' thought Bodie, as he dropped into the street, '– knowing the ground better than the other guy.' He was tempted to smile at the horrified expression on the assassin's face – an expression that stayed as Kodai checked and turned to see Doyle coming up behind him at an almost casual pace. There was nothing casual, though, in the way both agents trained their guns on the trapped man.

Keeping a level bead on the Russian's midriff, Bodie began to move in, alert for any sudden movement or the appearance of a concealed weapon, knowing that the element of surprise worked best when the chase seems to be over – that an enemy can be most deadly when appearing to accept defeat.

The surprise, when it came, wasn't from Kodai. Bodie had just enough time to register the roar of an engine, before a car erupted out of nowhere, heading straight for him. His leap was sheer instinct. It took him out of range of the front wheel by no more than a millimetre. He hit the ground, rolling, as the driver swerved towards Kodai and dropped speed. Doyle's shot whanged off the front mudguard, as Kodai wrenched open the passenger door and flung himself across the seat. With the door still flapping wildly, the car slewed away and screamed out of sight.

Bodie and Doyle leaned against the wall, panting, and watched it disappear. Bodie was the first to find his voice: 'I feel I know that guy.'

'Yeah,' Doyle's response was acid. 'If someone's just spent fifteen minutes trying to kill you, you do feel you know him ... funny that!'

His partner continued to look at the point where the car had gone out of sight. 'Not Kodai,' he said slowly. 'His driving instructor.'

Chapter Two

The house was ordinary – the word described it to perfection. An architect might have said that it possessed no distinguishing features or points of interest, that its façade was unexceptional, that there was nothing to particularly recommend it. Ordinary was a better term; ordinary and safe. The hundreds of people who passed it each day wouldn't have afforded the place a second glance. And that was what made it safe.

What went on behind the dully-painted front door and the discreetly-curtained windows, though, was far from ordinary. In CI5 parlance, 'safe house' wasn't a description of domestic normality: it was a technical term. A house the opposition didn't know about yet; a place where it was possible – for the time being at any rate – to be secure.

Cowley approved of the house; it merged with its background perfectly. He walked down the dim passageway that led to the room they'd taken Meredith to. As he reached the door, a man clad in a dark suit emerged, closing a black, medical bag.

'How is he, doctor?' queried Cowley.

'The wound itself is nothing – superficial.' The doctor paused, clearly disturbed. 'But his general condition ... Well, he looks as if he'd spent a year in a concentration camp.'

'Two years, in fact.' The doctor's head snapped up, but Cowley took no pleasure in administering the shock. To him, it was a brutal fact of life.

'Well,' the medical man continued, 'he needs complete rest and a high protein diet.'

Cowley nodded and made to enter the room. 'Oh, one other thing, sir. He's got hold of a bottle of whisky from somewhere. He shouldn't be drinking.'

'I'll see to it,' Cowley promised, then turned into the room to find Meredith struggling back into his shirt.

'The doctor says you're to have a complete rest.' From the way Cowley spoke, it was clear that he thought so too. As if he hadn't heard, the patient picked up a tie from a nearby chair and let it run through his fingers. His black tunic had been consigned to a convenient furnace.

'I haven't worn civilised clothes for two years,' The words were spoken almost dreamily.

'And this stuff will do you no good, Colin,' Cowley continued, hefting the whisky bottle that sat on a low table at the centre of the room. This time, Meredith heard. He all but snatched the bottle from Cowley's hand, poured a stiff measure into a glass and downed it in one. 'Something else I haven't had for a long time –' his voice hard, now. 'God how I used to crave for the taste of it.' He put the glass down and reached for his jacket.

Cowley looked shocked. 'You're not fit to go out, man.'

'Radouk has to be contacted,' Meredith retorted, 'assuming you want to go on with the deal.'

'I'm interested.' There was determination behind the words. 'But you can't go alone.'

'Look, George,' reasoned Meredith. 'Radouk's selling you one of the most valuable secrets in the history of espionage. He doesn't trust anyone – probably not even me! If I turn up with a couple of your goons breathing down my neck he'll read it as a double-cross. That's the mood he's in.'

'All right ...' Cowley was still reluctant. 'But the minute you're back, the doctor puts you under sedation. A full twenty-four hours. Agreed?'

Meredith lingered at the door, his silence giving consent. Then he emphasised: 'Just don't try to have me followed, George.'

*

Approaching the house, Bodie and Doyle saw Meredith disappearing into a taxi. He wasn't hurrying – and both men knew that he couldn't have left without Cowley's compliance – so they exchanged shrugs and went inside.

Cowley was waiting for them; and his mood wasn't altogether sweet.

'Congratulations,' he offered sourly. 'Two to one – and you lost him!'

The partners looked distinctly unapologetic. They knew that Cowley would have had time to sift the verbal report they'd given him as they drove back from the docks and that he'd be less concerned with the recent past than with what his next move should be. The reprimand was routine.

'I recognised his driver –' Bodie's contribution. 'Did some surveillance on him a couple of years ago. Jan Malenski. Pole. Came here during the war.'

The other two men looked blankly at him: surprised not to know the name if Bodie was familiar with it. The next name Bodie pulled out of the hat got a reaction, though.

'Well, how about Gregor Bhukarov. Ever heard of him?'

'Even my mum's heard of Bhukarov.' Doyle was right; there were very few people in the country who wouldn't respond to the name. Bhukarov's defection to the West had made headlines the world over.

Cowley made the connection: 'Of course,' he exclaimed, 'Malenski. He was one of the names Bhukarov gave us –'

'– after he defected,' Bodie finished his chief's sentence for him. 'Right. Among a lot of others. All KGB recruits, but low grade. I remember checking Malenski out.'

'And?' demanded Cowley.

'Nothing – till now.'

'So he doesn't know you.'

Bodie's look was eloquent: something akin to *Look, you might be the guv'nor, but I know how to do my job.*

All he said was: 'No.'

Cowley was indifferent to Bodie's hurt pride. His mind was elsewhere. Finally he said, 'He's the type Kodai might use if he didn't have much time to set up the hit ...' He pondered; then came to a decision. 'Very well, pull Malenski in. But before you do I've got two things to say. One – just because Kodai failed to kill Meredith today, don't under-estimate him. He's a formidable agent. Two ...' Here Cowley paused a moment and walked to the window, as if seeking the best way to say what was coming next. '... Two – remember the stakes we're playing for. This operation is vital.' His face was stern. 'Absolutely vital!'

George Cowley was a man with a well-developed sense of irony – and it would have amused him, though not for long, if he'd seen the thoroughly middle-class street, with its detached and semi-detached houses, where Meredith's taxi finally stopped. There was safety in anonymity, for sure; but there was safety in respectability, too. Even agents, Cowley might have reflected, have their life-styles.

Meredith paid off the cabbie, walked unhesitatingly to the front door of a house in the middle of the street and rang the bell. The door opened to admit him, without visible sign of anyone on the inside. He entered and walked straight across the hallway into a room. A man was sitting directly opposite the door. They faced each other, speechlessly; then Meredith held up his bandaged arm.

'You wouldn't win many coconuts, would you, Kodai?' The rhetorical question held more than a trace of anger.

The Russian said nothing. His gaze continued to hold Meredith's. Apart from the glitter of cold hostility in his eyes, the broad, Slavic face remained expressionless.

A further door opened and a slight, elegantly dressed man joined them. Meredith turned to the newcomer.

'It's a mess, Radouk.' He gestured angrily at Kodai. '*His* mess!'

This time, the Russian responded. '*You* moved in front of Cowley,' he spat. 'You're lucky I didn't blow your head off.'

Radouk waved a hand impatiently. The fiasco at the docks had been unfortunate, to say the least. Like Cowley, though, Radouk was a professional. Things had fouled up, but the conspiracy hadn't been exposed. Losing a battle was a setback; but the important task was to win the war.

He faced them – the Russian hit-man and the English traitor – viewing them as a chess-master might view the only two strong pieces left on his board. He must use them, he knew, with skill and care if he was to win the game – and this could be the most important game of his career!

'Recriminations are a luxury we don't have time for,' he said firmly. Then: 'Did they believe your story, Meredith?'

'Yeah, I think so,' said Meredith cautiously, trying to read Radouk's mind.

'And what is the first lesson an agent learns?' The question didn't beg an answer. Radouk waited, though, before continuing: 'If you've got a story, stick to it.'

'*Stick* to it?' Meredith shook his head. 'I'm not going back. It's too risky.'

'You must!' Radouk was accepting no argument. 'We must all take risks until the job is done ... and Cowley is dead!'

Chapter Three

It hadn't taken Bodie long to discover that since he'd run his check on Malenski, not much had changed in the man's life. He still lived in a slummy street of terraced houses, rarely leaving his room unless he had to and generally keeping the lowest of low profiles. His Russian masters knew he was not a man who could be allowed to act on his own initiative: he waited for orders, then carried them out to the letter. He could be trusted – but it was fear that kept him loyal.

Bodie eased his car into the back street and stopped long enough to let Doyle out, then he drove off. It was a routine they knew backwards: one man makes the approach, the other covers the back way out, and unless the quarry tunnels out, he's trapped.

Doyle rang Malenski's bell and waited. He could sense the face at an upstairs window, but showed no interest – just waited a little longer and rang again. Malenski wasn't there to hear the second ring; he was already in the alley behind his house, wheeling a motorbike along the narrow paving and heading for the main road. When he thought he was a safe distance from his back-gate, he straddled the bike, kicked it into life and accelerated towards the junction.

He'd gone no more than fifteen yards along the main street, when the bike began to lose power, then splutter. Malenski twisted the throttle desperately, but there was no answering surge of speed. He pulled over to the kerb, as the engine died and began kicking frantically at the start-lever. Behind him, a car door slammed.

'I think you've run out of juice.' Bodie watched the slow shock creep over the man's face. He gestured to the car with Doyle behind the wheel. 'But then you're going our way in any case – aren't you?' he continued pleasantly.

Malenski gazed from Bodie to Doyle and back again; then he gave the bike an awkward push to block Bodie's pursuit and started to run frantically down the street. Bodie watched him go – unmoving. Doyle, it was, who gave chase, taking off with a long squeal of tyres, reaching his man in a matter of seconds and swinging the bonnet on to the pavement so that Malenski ran full-tilt into it. He dropped – and stayed down on his face, as if afraid to look at his pursuers. When, finally, he did turn over, they were both looking down at him.

'Not very nice, is it Malenski? Being run down by a car.' Bodie's voice wasn't at all pleasant, now. 'I didn't enjoy it either.'

Malenski looked badly scared. His mouth was trembling uncontrollably and he kept raising his hand slightly, flinching, as if to protect his face. When he spoke, there was a false bravado in his words: 'I won't talk,' he whined. 'You won't make me talk.'

Bodie and Doyle exchanged a look. It wasn't a matter of *whether* the man would give them the information they wanted: just a matter of how quickly.

Doyle loked down at the terrified man. 'Come on,' he said. Together, the partners half-lifted, half-pushed Malenski into the car.

The distaste showed on George Cowley's face as he watched Meredith pour himself a gigantic Scotch and down half of it; though if Meredith noticed the disapproval, he obviously didn't care. He took a second slug of whisky before saying: 'Radouk sends you his regards.'

'Really?' There was a wealth of scepticism in Cowley's reply.

'You're the only one he trusts, George. He'll deal with you and you alone.'

Cowley remained unimpressed. 'Should I feel flattered?' he asked wryly.

Meredith shrugged. 'The point is – are you willing?'

He was playing things as coolly as he knew how, trying not to make Cowley suspicious by being too insistent, but keeping A-squad's chief on the hook. He knew that to blow the cover of a double-agent at the very top of British Intelligence would be an enormous coup for Cowley. He also knew that beyond any desire Cowley might have for personal glory, lay a fierce determination to cut out the cancer that threatened the entire Intelligence network ... for that was how Cowley regarded a traitor – as something malignant. For Radouk's plan to work, though, Cowley had to be persuaded that he – and no one else – could wield the knife.

Are you willing? Cowley knew that there could be no other way. Even so, he remained wary. 'That would depend on what arrangements Radouk has in mind,' he said.

Eagerly, Meredith seized on Cowley's lead: 'There's a disused RAF base near Manley.'

'Yes, I know it.'

'At noon tomorrow, Radouk will arrive there in a chopper. Alone. You make the exchange. Radouk flies out. End of story.'

Still Cowley had reservations. 'Kodai has a different ending in mind, I suspect.'

'That's our problem,' Meredith knew he was home and dry now that they were discussing details. 'We've got to seal off that base so even Kodai can't get through.'

'That'll take a lot of men, a lot of movement,' objected Cowley. 'It's tantamount to sending Kodai a formal invitation.'

Meredith was prepared for this – it was an obvious flaw in his tactics, but it was essential that things should be set up his way. As casually as he could, he said, 'He may know already. Radouk's own security isn't what it was.'

It seemed a flimsy explanation, but there was no argument from Cowley; just a curt: 'Very well.'

Now came the clincher. Meredith judged his words

with care. 'There's one other condition, George. You meet Radouk alone. If anyone else approaches closer than five hundred yards, it'll be taken as a breach of faith.'

'From what you say,' Cowley retorted, 'I'm surprised that Radouk feels himself in a position to make conditions.' It was a clever objection – and an important one. A man trying to defect – a man on the run, with killers after him and nothing to trade with but secrets locked away in his own head – lived in a terrible limbo, neither on one side nor the other. Until his deal had been accepted and the information traded for political asylum, or the papers and other paraphernalia needed to start a new life under a new name, he was at risk twenty-four hours a day. Such a man had little enough to bargain with; and he was likely to do exactly as he was told.

Again, Meredith judged his words carefully. 'He's very twitchy. He was relying on his "mole" – his man at the top. And the man refused him.'

Cowley considered. 'When was this?' he asked.

'Four days ago. And thank God he did refuse.'

'Your ticket out of jail and mine to a top double-agent,' Cowley agreed.

'An agent,' added Meredith, 'Radouk now has no qualms about betraying.'

'For a price,' added Cowley.

'For a price, yes. But cheap at that price.' It was an unnecessary reminder: they both knew that for the kind of information Radouk had to offer, no price was too great. It was obvious, now, that Cowley intended to pay the price and find his traitor. The atmosphere in the room was relaxed. Both men knew that a bargain had been struck. A new identity for a turncoat's name – a life for a life.

Meredith was well pleased. His satisfaction turned to mild concern, though, as the doctor entered the room and looked at him meaningfully.

'What's this, George?'

'Twenty-four hours under sedation,' Cowley replied. 'Remember?'

The mutinous look on Meredith's face gave way to resignation. 'Anything you say, George.' He allowed the doctor to lead him out of the room.

After the door was securely closed, Cowley crossed to a phone and dialled a three-digit number. 'Records?' he asked brusquely, 'Send up everything you've got on a Jan Malenski.' He replaced the receiver and stood there deep in thought, not moving, barely conscious, any more, of his surroundings. Before records sent the file up to him, he had plans to make.

Lying on the bed, Meredith watched the doctor remove a syringe and a glass phial containing clear liquid from his bag. He struggled to get the correct note of mild fear into his voice when he said, 'Haven't you got any pills?'

The doctor turned. 'Mr Cowley said ...'

'Look,' Meredith cut him short. 'Where I've been for the last two years, they do things to you with needles.'

The medic hesitated. He had his orders ... but what this man had been through didn't bear thinking about. He persisted, but weakly: 'An injection's much more effective ...'

'Please, doctor!' Meredith let a touch more fear into his voice – an edge of desperation – and the doctor relented. 'Oh, very well,' he sighed. He returned the syringe to the bag, taking out instead a bottle of pills, then shaking three of the tablets into his palm.

'Take three now,' he said, 'and I'll come in and have a look at you in five or six hours.'

'Thanks.' Meredith took a glass of water from the bedside table, tossed the pills back into his mouth and gulped at the water. The doctor watched this until he was satisfied that his patient would shortly be dead to the world, then he crossed to the door. 'Sleep well,' he said as he went out.

As the door closed, so Meredith put his hand to his mouth and spat out the pills he'd been keeping securely under his tongue. His immediate plans didn't include being unconscious for twenty-four hours. To begin with, he'd got a report to make. He glanced over at the phone, listening to make sure there were no sounds from outside the door ...

A thin blade of light lanced through the shutters that hid the interrogation room from the world. Outside, dawn was edging low, purple clouds with silver. The streets were empty apart from the occasional vagrant with no home to go to, or shiftworkers making for their daytime beds. Inside, Malenski sat in a stiff-backed chair, his hands resting on a plain deal table. He was trying to look composed, but it wasn't working. His eyes betrayed fear: but there was a kind of stubborn courage in his voice. Cowley, together with Doyle and Bodie, stood over him.

'I will tell you nothing.' The hands twitched slightly on the table, betraying him, and he pulled them quickly into his lap.

Cowley was being almost kindly: speaking in a soft, deceptive tone. 'I haven't asked you anything yet, Laddie,' he observed.

'You'll get nothing from me,' repeated Malenski, his eyes travelling round the circle of faces.

'Get?' Cowley appeared genuinely confused. 'I've come to give you something ... haven't I Bodie?'

Bodie nodded in agreement as Cowley picked up a file lying on the table, took a photograph out of it, paused for effect, then handed it to Malenski, whose face had taken on a look of complete bewilderment. The look quickly changed to one of horror.

'Where did you get this?' – a strained whisper.

Without bothering to reply, Cowley reclaimed the photo and handed it to Doyle. 'He takes after his mother, don't you think?'

'Spit and image,' agreed Doyle. It was a cruel game and the three CI5 men knew it. But it had to be played. Each man had his own price; and each man had his own breaking-point. They knew enough about Malenski from Bodie's original check on the man to guess where his weak point would lie – and the guess was a good one.

Cowley extracted another photograph from the folder and handed it to the prisoner, deliberately giving the man no time to gather himself.

'Your sister Sonia and her husband and children – in the park in Warsaw. Taken last summer ...' Remorselessly, Cowley whipped a third photo from the file and pushed it under Malenski's nose. 'Your Uncle Peter – in national costume. Most picturesque.'

Blow after blow ... Cowley was a past master at this sort of pressure. He knew just how much force to apply, just how much to leave unsaid. On seeing the last snapshot, Malenski's nerve broke. Fear, anger, anxiety – all these were in his voice: 'Why are you showing me these? Where did you get them?'

'We've known about you for years, Jan, so we made it our business to find out about your background.' Cowley was going for the kill, now. He added, 'It wasn't very difficult, was it, Bodie?'

'Like falling off a log,' agreed Bodie.

Cowley continued rapidly. 'We found out all about your cousin, who works in the steelyard, and your sister, and your widowed mother, and all the others – just in case one day you were in a position to help us. And today is that day.'

The last five words were uttered with cruel emphasis; Malenski had no doubts about their meaning, and no doubts about Cowley's seriousness. But he knew that he had more than just Cowley to worry about. He was in a vicious trap – on one side CI5, on the other his own people – and he couldn't expect a shred of pity from either.

'If I help you,' he whimpered, 'Kodai will have my family eliminated.'

'If you help me the only elimination, as you put it, will be of Kodai himself,' said Cowley; and for just a second, it seemed that he might be trying persuasion: offering reassurances, not issuing threats.

'It's not a risk I choose to take, Mr Cowley.'

'In that case,' came the reply, 'I have no choice either. I will have your family in Poland incriminated as Western agents.' The trap was sprung: and Malenski felt its steel jaws bite. Still he struggled, though.

'No one will believe it,' he said, trying to force some scorn into his tone.

Cowley knew he was facing a defeated man. 'My people will ensure the evidence against them is incontrovertible,' he replied. The trap bit deeper. Malenski felt the pain, and like a wounded animal reacted with fury. He flung himself at his tormentor, reaching for the throat, trying to hit back in the only way left to him. Bodie and Doyle were on to him in a flash, throwing him back into the chair and pinning him there.

'You bastard!' Malenski shrieked. 'You're like Kodai – you use people, innocent people, old people, anyone, to get what you want.'

Cowley wasn't in a mood to justify himself. His was a dirty business – it was often necessary to use dirty methods. In Cowley's war there was little place for honour or fancy notions of 'fair play'. He believed his cause to be a just one, though, in the same way that he believed his methods to be less savage, less careless of human suffering than those of the other side.

'I do try to get what I want,' he admitted coolly, 'but I'm not like Kodai. I look after the people I use. Help me – and I'll protect your family. Refuse me – and I'll do what Kodai would do; what Kodai probably will do, anyway, once you're no longer of use to him.'

At least there was a bargain to be made here – and Malenski could see that. He slumped miserably in the chair – utterly broken. Cowley gave him a moment to accept the defeat, then he said gently, 'You know where Kodai is?' There was a pause, then Malenski nodded, keeping his face towards the floor so that no one would have the satisfaction of seeing the wetness in his eyes.

Later the same day, Bodie and Doyle left the house and made for the car parked at the kerb. Malenski had given them all the detail they needed: now it was up to them to make sure that Kodai was taken cleanly. Cowley, walking with them to the car, was particularly anxious that there should be no slip-ups.

'I want Kodai alive –' he stressed the word '– and anyone else there is with him. Understood?' He waited for a nod of agreement, then went on: 'Just play it by the book. Especially you, Bodie!'

Bodie shot him a look of wounded innocence: *What, me?* Then he climbed in next to Doyle, started the motor, and moved off at an exaggeratedly sedate pace. Cowley's instructions had set the pattern for the operation, just as they always did. Bodie and Doyle would always trust their chief's ability to sum up a situation, make the best decision and issue the orders. If he sometimes seemed to ask for the near-impossible – well, that they could manage. The truly impossible took a little longer.

By the same token, they knew – and Cowley knew – that once the action started, the partners would have to play things by ear. No two jaunts ever followed a pattern. It was important to expect the unexpected; it was even more important to come out of the operation with a whole skin. If any two operatives could bring Kodai in alive, they were Bodie and Doyle; but if things fouled up – anything could happen.

Cowley watched the car disappear along the street; then he returned to the anonymous interior of the safe house. As he entered the room that served as his office, one among a bank of telephones was ringing insistently. He strode over and lifted the handset: 'Cowley,' he said tersely.

'I thought it was time we had a talk, Mr Cowley.' The voice was instantly recognisable. Kodai! It continued: '... at a safe distance this time.'

Cowley smiled to himself. 'You're maybe thinking of the last wee chat we had?' His Lowland Scottish burr was deceptively soft – also, he was playing for time. As he spoke, he was lifting another, nearby, phone and dialling swiftly.

Kodai was distinctly unamused by Cowley's remark. 'I still have the scar.' The voice was openly hostile. 'A constant reminder of how little your word is worth.'

'About as much as yours,' remarked Cowley, unrepentantly, and punched a button on the second phone. In Bodie's car, the R/T bleeped. Doyle lifted the mike, snapped down a button and was just in time to catch Cowley's next statement: 'You had a gun too, Kodai. I was just quicker.'

'Happily, not quick enough.' Guessing who the other speaker was, Bodie and Doyle exchanged a significant look.

Knowing that his agents would be listening in by this time, Cowley brought the parrying banter to a close. 'I presume you haven't called me to reminisce about the past,' he said sardonically, then snatched half a second to hiss 'I'll keep him talking' into the receiver that connected with Bodie's R/T.

'Indeed no,' replied Kodai. 'I want to talk about the present ... and the future.'

The agents had reached a clear stretch of road a mile or so from the address Malenski had given them. Doyle reckoned that Cowley could manage to keep Kodai on the phone – and therefore distracted – for another three or four minutes. It would give them an advantage that might not come as easily again. 'Go!' he yelled; and

Bodie floored the accelerator, leaving behind him a couple of ounces of rubber and a handful of startled pedestrians.

Cowley continued to lead Kodai on, knowing that his men would be aware of what was happening.

'I don't think we have too much to talk about, Kodai,' he said, 'but I'm prepared to listen.'

'I want Radouk!' A flat statement – and one that Cowley had expected. He'd known that this would be the approach, and he was interested to see how Kodai would mount his argument – what terms he would offer. He might have been even more interested, though, in the fact that behind him a door had been opened, stealthily, while Meredith listened to the twin conversation Cowley was having ... a door that was now being closed with infinite care.

'I haven't got Radouk,' Cowley parried. Not five miles away, Radouk smiled thinly as he heard Cowley's voice crackle over the wire. Kodai noticed the smile, but had no time to dwell on the amusing aspect of the deception – nor had Meredith who, in his room in the safe house, had carefully lifted the extension telephone in time to hear Kodai say: 'But you can get him. At noon tomorrow. At RAF Manley. My information is ... comprehensive. I could, for instance, kill Meredith any time I like. But Meredith is not important. Radouk is.'

Meredith lowered the extension millimetre by millimetre; then he picked up a phone that would give him an outside line and began to dial ... at about the same time as the agents' car slewed round a corner cutting up a furniture van, a motor-cyclist who just managed to stay upright and a learner-driver who gawped wide-eyed at the four-wheel drift that took Bodie and Doyle across his road-space, then out of sight in a wrenching squeal of roasting tyres.

Meanwhile, Cowley was holding to his task of keeping Kodai occupied. 'Why should I hand Radouk over to you?' he demanded.

The answer was unconvincing: 'You and I are opposite sides of the same coin, Cowley. But it is an old, devalued coin. It belongs to a war which is over.'

As he was speaking, another phone, on the far side of the room, started to ring. Radouk moved to it, quickly.

'Buy Radouk's information,' continued Kodai,' and you start that war again. Look to the future, Cowley.'

On the other phone, Radouk listened, but uttered no word. A second was all it took for him to absorb Meredith's information; then he strode across the room signalling to the other man. It was a moment before Kodai got the message. 'He is a traitor,' he said to Cowley. 'He deserves his punishment.'

'I'm looking for a traitor too, Kodai,' observed Cowley, sensing that the conversation could be prolonged further. There was a second's silence: then a click as the line went dead. Cowley frowned, then put the phone down with a puzzled look. Something was wrong – but his agents weren't answering the R/T call that he immediately put out. They must, he reasoned, be in the grounds of Kodai's house by now and there was no way he could help them. They were on their own.

Under cover provided by a thick screen of bushes, Bodie watched the house, sensing his partner's arrival as he leapt down from the garden wall and made a low, crouching run that brought him alongside. They waited, to be sure that no one had seen them, then sprinted to new cover nearer the house. Again they waited; then Doyle moved on, at top speed, to flatten himself against the wall of the house. Bodie remained to give support, as Doyle edged up to a french window.

Nearby, an engine gunned mightily, then a car erupted from a garage at the side of the house, the driver going up through the gears at relentless speed and spraying gravel in a fantail arc. It braked ferociously, then boomed out into the street, giving the two agents no time to do anything but watch helplessly as it disappeared from sight. Holstering their guns, they looked down the now empty street and then at each other. Round two to the opposition.

'I hate flashy drivers,' said Bodie.

Cowley paced quietly down the corridor to Meredith's room and eased open the door. The curtains were drawn, a muted light filtering through the material and smudging objects with deep grey shadows. Meredith lay in bed, eyes closed, breathing deeply and evenly. Cowley watched for a brief spell, then closed the door with exaggerated care.

Chapter Four

This time, Cowley knew, his agents weren't to blame. But something had gone wrong – again – and there had to be a post-mortem. It was seriously worrying that the opposition should seem to be always one jump ahead of them. Things had reached the stage where one piece of information, one advantage, could well prove crucial – or fatal. It wasn't enough to think one move ahead; it was necessary to *be* one move ahead.

'Something must have tipped Kodai off' – Cowley was not so much stating the obvious as thinking aloud.

'He could have had a man outside somewhere,' offered Bodie, then continued, '– but we didn't see anyone.' *And we would have* ... that part of his sentence was left unsaid, but it was clearly implied: and Cowley accepted the implication. If there wasn't a look-out posted, then Kodai's ability to avoid capture was doubly puzzling, doubly worrying. Unless the Russian had second-sight, or a crystal ball, then he was getting his information from more human – more sinister – sources.

Cowley considered a moment. 'I want Meredith moved – out of harm's way,' he said.

'There's number twelve ...' Doyle named another safe house.

'Good enough,' agreed Cowley, 'but one of you stays with him – all the time! Take it in shifts.'

'Playing nursemaid!' Bodie was obviously disgusted by the idea.

'Obeying orders, Brodie,' snapped Cowley in a voice that clearly stated he would stand for none of Bodie's well-known unorthodox behaviour during this critical time. The pair detected the hardness in their chief's tone and made for the door. Cowley's tone didn't soften as he said: 'And make absolutely sure you're not followed.

I don't want any more ...' he paused to make sure the next word would have the desired effect, 'mistakes!'

The agents left – suitably chastened. After they had gone, Cowley moved to the telephone; as he dialled, his expression bore signs of strain. Things were not going to plan – and that always disturbed Cowley greatly. Before the meeting tomorrow, many plans had to be made: plans that would leave no room for even the slightest error. Error led to failure ... usually to death.

'This is Cowley, CI5,' he said into the phone. 'Put me through to the Air Commodore, please.'

Bodie and Doyle didn't feel that they'd made any mistakes during their two brushes with Kodai: they'd played things according to the book – or, at least, according to *their* book. The fact that they had lost out twice pleased them no more than it pleased Cowley. They had their pride to think of – to say nothing of their skins!

Moving Meredith to a new address was a simple enough operation; even so, they determined to take every precaution. As their car passed a major intersection, Bodie trod on the brake and brought the vehicle to a halt. Doyle clambered out, walked back the few yards to the crossroads, looked both ways, then returned to the car.

Bodie let the clutch in snappily before his partner had properly closed the door. 'Anything?' he asked.

'Clear,' replied Doyle as the car roared along the street.

Meredith smiled faintly. 'That's the third time,' he observed. 'Kodai's really got you worried.'

'Kodai's got Cowley worried,' corrected Bodie. *And when Cowley's worried – everyone worries*, he might have added. That was why the partners were using Cowley's 'book' for this particular jaunt, rather than their own re-written version of the rules. There would be no mistakes this time; accidents, perhaps, but no mistakes.

'Where are we going?' Meredith queried.

'Safe house,' informed Bodie.

Meredith gave a short, bitter laugh. 'Safe' house, to him, meant more imprisonment; he was beginning to feel edgy, hemmed-in. 'And when I got out of Phnom Pehn,' he said sourly, 'I really thought I was coming back to freedom.'

Bodie wasn't impressed by the complaint. 'In the circumstances,' he suggested, 'I wouldn't complain.'

Meredith sneered. 'What the hell do you know about it?'

There was no reply for a second. Bodie swung the car into the kerb outside number twelve, and cut the engine. Then he turned to face Meredith. 'I know all about it, Meredith.' He regarded the man coldly. 'We all do. Only some of us don't keep *talking* about it. Right?'

Meredith held Bodie's icy glare as he got out of the car. For a brief, electric moment they faced up to each other on the pavement, then Meredith's eyelid flickered and he dropped his gaze. Bodie accepted the surrender. 'Come on,' he said. They began to walk towards the front door. Doyle slipped into the driver's seat and drove off down the road.

'So you've got first shift, have you?' There was still a trace of aggression in the voice.

It was Bodie's turn to sneer now. He opened the door and ushered Meredith inside. 'I lost the toss,' he observed dryly.

Doyle had called 'tails' – he always called 'tails' and he always seemed to win – a tiny defeat for the law of averages. While Bodie was doing the baby-sitting, he had gone back to the scene of Kodai's second escape. He knew the house would be deserted: no one would make the mistake of going within miles of a place once its cover had been blown. But Kodai had left in one hell of a hurry and it was more than likely that he'd only had time to clear up in the most perfunctory way. With a couple of CI5 men breathing down your neck, you don't hang about to do the spring-cleaning; and Doyle knew that sometimes the most insignificant object could turn out to be an essential lead.

He'd gone through the house thoroughly, but Kodai was a professional too. He'd left nothing that could provide any clue to his whereabouts – or his plans. Doyle returned to the main room and looked around for the last time. Nothing. He was about to leave, when he noticed the second phone. Walking over to it, he checked the number, then lifted the receiver. Not an extension – a second line; two lines in one house ... and Kodai had been speaking to Cowley when the tip-off had been given. *It doesn't take a genius* ... thought Doyle as he replaced the handset.

Bodie yawned; then he yawned again. There were times, he reflected, when CI5 seemed positively tame, especially for a man who had seen action with the paras. Then he thought again. No, okay, it wasn't tame; in fact it was often distinctly hairy; and the stakes were very, very high. But right now he could have used a little action. Playing nanny to a whiner like Meredith wasn't his idea of a fun way to pass the time. In fact ...

His train of thought broke, instantly, when he heard the faint noise from somewhere in the house. He listened intently in case it should come again; then he moved silently into the passageway between the main rooms and padded down to the bedroom. He eased the door open a fraction: enough to see that Meredith was still there, lying on the bed and, to all intents and purposes, fast asleep.

Back in the living-room, Bodie paused again. The sound was almost inaudible: a scratching, accompanied by a slight squeak. Gun in hand, Bodie went back into the corridor. The noise came again: more clearly this time, from the kitchen directly opposite. The sound of wood rubbing against wood, the thready squeak of a small pulley. The kitchen window was being opened inch by inch.

Bodie gathered himself, then crashed into the room, deliberately dropping sideways as his gun came up to take a bead on the man who was half-way through the window. The intruder's gunshot came a split second after Bodie's, sounding almost like an echo. The bullet smacked into the door-frame, taking out a great chunk of wood at about the point where Bodie's head would have been but for the sideways roll. There was no chance for a second try. Bodie's shot had taken the gunman full in the chest, slapping him back against the sash-window; the impact held him for an instant, spread-eagled against the blood-spattered glass. Then he slumped into the room, his legs twisted and trapped by the sill.

Bodie checked him to make sure: but he knew the man would be dead; at that range, a .38 cupro-nickel slug would seriously damage an elephant! He kicked the gun across the kitchen floor – and in the same instant heard the sound of someone moving from the living-room towards the room where Meredith lay sleeping.

He'd travelled a foot or so towards the corridor, when a gun opened up from somewhere outside the window. Bodie dropped. Automatic fire! A machine pistol, maybe an automatic rifle. These guys were serious! He glanced up to see the wall on the far side of the corridor being ploughed into a moon-scape of smashed plaster and lath as the stream of bullets struck. The door-frame had almost disintegrated and shards of wood whirred about the room amid the plaster-dust. The line of fire was directly above Bodie's head, through the door and into the wrecked corridor wall. Anything crossing that line would be chewed to a pulp. Helpless, Bodie lay alongside the dead man, covered in fragments of glass and wood-splinters and cursed his luck as the remorseless ribbon of lead whined through the air a couple of feet above him.

Meredith had come awake with the first shot. For a moment, he was confused: why would they be getting him out? Then confusion changed to a faint, needling fear. Through the half-light in the darkened bedroom, he saw a figure slip through the door. The light clicked on.

Kodai's gun was levelled at a point directly between Meredith's eyes – eyes that now showed naked terror. He opened his mouth to speak – plead, beg, anything to delay the moment when the bullet would rip into him, but Kodai was in no mood for talk. He steadied his aim and fired full into the terrified face across the room. Meredith's body twisted and crashed back against the wall, his arms coming up in a grotesque parody of someone surrendering. Then he crumpled.

In the same second, the automatic fire stopped. Kodai stepped into the corridor, braced himself against the wall and trained his gun on the room where Bodie had lain trapped. As he emerged, he'd be a sitting target. It was a fact that occurred to Bodie, too. He wasn't at all unhappy that the automatic had stopped digging a crater in the far wall; but he knew there had to be a reason. Crouched on his haunches, he waited for the next move. Then he heard the automatic start up again: short, chopping rhythms as the gunman seeded bullets over a wide field of fire – only this time they weren't coming through the window behind him.

The new target was Doyle's car – he'd got half-way down the street before he'd seen the gunman perched on a vantage point on the far side of the roadway. To turn the car would have been fatal; instead, Doyle stood on the brakes and slewed the car broadside to give some cover. Automatic fire raked the bodywork, smashing through the thin panels as Doyle catapulted from the driver's seat on the safe side and tried to gain a sight of his attacker.

In the kitchen, Bodie heard the commotion, guessed what was happening, and made for the door. Kodai also heard and decided not to hang around: for all he knew, half of CI5 could be on the doorstep, together with Special Branch and the Seventh Cavalry. His job was done – Bodie would keep.

He yanked open a window at the far end of the corridor just as Bodie came clear of the kitchen door and was through and into the street soon enough for Bodie's snap shot to miss its mark. The gunman in the street covered Kodai as he raced for their nearby car, rattling off a few rounds at Bodie as he appeared at the window. This gave Doyle his chance. Setting his legs in a solid stance, he steadied his handgun and fired four times in rapid succession. The gunman went down in a welter of nerveless limbs and blood just as Kodai reached the car. Wrenching open the door he emptied his gun in Doyle's direction, sending the CI5 man back into cover, then leapt behind the wheel and sent the car screeching along the street in a crazy half-controlled racing start. Doyle straightened up, took careful aim at the tyres, and fired twice before he heard the hammer fall on an empty chamber. Then, seeing that his bullets hadn't found their mark, he sprinted over to join Bodie at their car. Ironically, three of the tyres had been shredded in the crossfire.

Gasping for breath, the partners looked at each other. Twin looks of utter disgust. Then Bodie exclaimed: 'Meredith!' They reached the bedroom door together and stopped short. Meredith's corpse was lying half on the floor, half on the bed, his arms still extended in a gesture of defeat. The sheet directly under him bore a wide, ever-spreading bloodstain.

Without looking away from the body, Bodie said, 'How the hell did they know he was here?'

Doyle had spotted the telephone on the far side of the bed. Telephones! It was certainly a day for two and two resulting in a neat answer of four!

'Somewhere,' Ray Doyle observed wryly, 'someone was waiting for a call ... from him.' He gestured at the bed.

Bodie shook his head sorrowfully. 'I think I prefer Buzzby,' he said.

'You led Kodai straight to Meredith!' Cowley was white with anger. Events were going against him; *luck* was going against him. Two failures to capture Kodai when he was well within their clutches – and now this! Meredith gunned down when he was in the care of CI5's top agents.

Bodie was angry, too. He knew damn well that he and his partner hadn't made any mistakes. 'We weren't followed!' He came as close to raising his voice as he dared. Old army habits died hard, and he wasn't in the habit of yelling at a superior officer. But he had no intention of being blamed for this particular foul-up. He was a good operative and he knew it – knew his limitations, too. Sometimes he'd take short-cuts, ignore the book of rules in order to get something done or lean on a villain harder than he should. On this occasion, he'd obeyed orders to the letter. Something deeper than mere human failing lay behind Meredith's murder.

Cowley was unrepentant. 'Weren't you?' he asked tartly. 'Then how the hell did Kodai locate number twelve? Clairvoyance?'

It was time for Doyle to say something. He spoke quietly, but what he said stopped the brewing row stone dead: 'It could have been Meredith, Sir.' Cowley looked at him speechlessly. Doyle went on, justifying what he'd said: 'There was a phone in his room.'

There was silence as Cowley turned away. His expression was thoughtful – but more than that. He had the look of a man who is deciding what line to take: how to play a poker hand, or what words to use for an important policy statement. He made the decision and turned back to Doyle. 'There are times Doyle,' he said carefully, 'when you show remarkable intelligence.' He waited for Doyle to register pleasure at this, then continued, '... but this is not one of them! Why would

Meredith use the phone to summon his own executioner?'

The pleasure left Doyle's face to be replaced by anger, then resignation. 'Perhaps,' he offered flippantly, 'he was just a poor judge of character.'

Cowley's face clouded; noticing, Bodie chipped in: 'The fact remains, Sir: there's no way we were followed.' The phone rang before Cowley had a chance to come back at him. He snatched it up and spoke his name.

'Good afternoon, Mr Cowley.' – Kodai's voice, unmistakably. Cowley listened intently as the Russian gloated. 'I warned you. *Now* will you be sensible and give me Radouk?'

'I'll make no deals with you, Kodai,' rasped Cowley.

The Russian's voice was almost unctuous: 'If you won't give me Radouk, Cowley, I shall have to take him.'

'You may try. That's your privilege.'

'When you meet Radouk tomorrow at Manley, I'll be there,' Kodai promised.

'That should make for an interesting exchange of views,' – Cowley's tone held a different sort of promise.

'Possibly.' Now it was Kodai's turn to sound angry. 'But strictly two-way. Radouk won't get the chance to utter a word!'

Chapter Five

The place hadn't been used for more than thirty years. Once, Lancasters had rumbled down the concrete runways and hauled themselves ponderously into the sky – plane after plane in an unending procession, until the night air had crackled and boomed with the sound of their great engines – vast formations headed for the dense, industrial complex of the Ruhr, carrying their cargoes of bombs and their crews of boys, most of whom seemed hardly out of their teens. Few of them saw more than ten sorties; the losses were appalling – as they were for the fighter pilots who piloted their Spits and Hurricanes into the mild, blue English skies as the invaders droned in. There had been many deaths, many moments of high drama. Now a weatherbeaten sign was the only reminder of those heroic days. Hanging askew from the gate, it announced: 'RAF MANLEY – KEEP OUT – MOD PROPERTY'. Today, though, for the first time in a long time, the place was to see more drama – and possibly more deaths!

Cowley's car raced down the weed-infested runway, past wrecked Nissen huts and tangled rolls of barbed wire, to come to rest near a vast hangar at the centre of the airfield. He got out and spent a moment looking round – sizing up the possible angles of approach – then entered the hangar. By the time he'd satisfied himself that he knew the layout, Bodie and Doyle had arrived.

'The men all here?' he asked.

'Sir!' – a military response from Bodie.

'Good. Now: precisely at noon, a helicopter will touch down ...' Cowley pointed to a spot some fifty feet in front of the hangar '... here. Radouk will get out and walk into this hangar where I will be waiting.

'After two or three minutes he will come out again,

get back into his helicopter and the helicopter will take off. In all, a stopover of less than ten minutes. And during that time –' his voice hardened, '– Kodai will try to kill him. So I want the perimeter of this field sewn up so tight a gnat can't get at us!'

'Knee-deep in dead insects already, Sir,' said Bodie confidently, handing Cowley a pair of binoculars. Cowley took them and scanned the perimeter. CI5 men were visible at all the key points, looking outwards away from the field and all of them armed.

'Good!' Cowley handed the glasses back. 'Patrol the immediate approaches to the airfield too. Roads, tracks, paths – I want them all covered. Kodai will come. I know it.'

No one was doubting that. In fact, it was something that had been on Bodie's mind for some time – that, and the fact that his Chief would be facing Radouk without any kind of back-up. All the rule books – even Bodie's – had something to say about a situation like that: they said it was crazy!

'You'll be alone with Radouk, Sir,' he stressed, 'no one else within five hundred yards. I don't like it.'

Cowley was adamant. '*I* don't like it, Bodie!' Then he added sharply, 'And even less do I like having my orders questioned.' There was no time for further discussion: Cowley's R/T began to bleep urgently; things were beginning to move.

'Right,' he prompted, 'clear off, both of you. I want no one within five hundred yards of me from now on. And I mean *nobody* – it doesn't matter who it is or what the circumstances are! Second – in absolutely no circumstances whatsoever is a shot to be fired until further orders. And anybody who disobeys will spend the rest of his life watching Russian trawlers in the Outer Hebrides!'

Bodie and Doyle were in the car and moving before the last words left their chief's mouth. It was Bodie who offered a parting shot: 'Nice to feel wanted ...' Then they were gunning the car across the airfield. Cowley moved to his own car and picked up the R/T. 'Touch-down in ten minutes,' he warned, checking his own wrist-watch. 'Stand by as from now, Air Commodore. Over ...'

Just outside the perimeter fence was a line of thick scrub – bushes, saplings, a tangle of thorny undergrowth – that gave way after a few yards to a dense wood. Bodie and Doyle took up a position beyond the scrub, but short of the trees so that they could still keep the airfield in view. They had drawn their guns and thumbed the safety catches off; and though they spoke to each other, their eyes were never still: travelling over the shadowy entrances to the wood, the paths between the trees, the nearby bushes.

'I'm quite looking forward to seeing Kodai again.' – This from Bodie.

Doyle's reply was equally casual: 'Oh yeah? Can't say that I am.'

'He's not such a bad sort,' Bodie joked. 'Bit careless with firearms and motor vehicles, I'll concede –'

'But he loves children and animals ... yeah, I know,' Doyle finished acidly. Then he said, 'Maybe he won't show.'

'He'll show. Fifty says he'll show!'

Doyle didn't take the bet; instead, he looked skyward as the unmistakable *whap-whap-whap* of a helicopter became audible. It was just a dot in the sky, but closing fast from the west. The partners watched for a second, then turned their attention to the woods. 'So where the hell is Kodai?' asked Bodie. The humour had gone from his voice.

Cowley had spotted the chopper from where he stood at the entrance to the hangar. He fixed his eyes on it as it closed on his position, then hovered almost directly overhead, making no attempt to land.

Doyle risked a look backwards. 'He's having a good long look.'

'Bloody advertising, I'd call it,' agreed Bodie, turning to watch for an instant. Then both men whipped round as they sensed rather than heard a movement in the undergrowth just on the fringe of the trees.

A few twigs swayed and there was an accompanying rustle. The only other sound was a dull *click* as Ray Doyle cocked his gun. Then Bodie appeared to relax slightly, letting his gun waver. There was just too much noise, he thought, for this to be Kodai – unless the Russian had suddenly developed a death-wish. Another loud rustle, a swaying of branches pushed aside, and a figure stepped into the clearing. He was in his late sixties, wore the greasy tatters of a dark suit, together with a ruined pair of plimsolls and sported a gigantic, verminous-looking beard.

He stood there for a moment, taking in the levelled guns and the tense expressions behind them. Then: 'Are you boys aware you're trespassing?' the tramp asked politely.

Doyle was too surprised to laugh. 'We've got permission,' he said, feeling a bit like a kid caught scrumping.

The tramp persisted: 'Are you sure about that?'

This time, Doyle managed a small grin. 'Quite sure.'

'Who from?' This character wasn't giving up!

'The Ministry of Defence,' Bodie assured him. 'It's all been cleared.'

The tramp regarded them suspiciously for a few seconds, then came to a decision. 'All right,' he said primly, 'as long as you've got permission, I don't mind.' As he turned to go back into the wood, a thought struck him: 'And I hope you've got licences for those guns of yours ...' Then he was gone.

The agents exchanged a look – not sure whether to laugh or groan. Behind them, the helicopter landed and a figure emerged, walking slowly towards the hangar.

Apart from a few shafts of light from windows high in the roof, the hangar was in a gloomy half-light. The man who had alighted from the chopper stood in the far doorway: featureless. a silhouette. He waited, then spoke: 'Cowley ... *Cowley!*' The name echoed in the arched roof; and as the echoes died, Cowley appeared, a second silhouette, at the other entrance to the hangar. He took a couple of paces forward, then stopped as the other man began to approach him, moving into a patch of light where he stopped rather like a stage magician perfecting a trick and waiting for his applause. The coarse, Slavic features remained expressionless ... Kodai stood in the column of sunlight, his gun trained on Cowley's midriff, and enjoyed the moment.

The head of A-squad hefted the briefcase he was carrying and took a couple more steps towards his opponent. The gun jerked. 'I told you it would be a two-way conversation, Cowley,' gloated the Russian. 'What's in the briefcase?'

'What Radouk asked for,' came the reply. 'A brand new British passport and two hundred thousand pounds in used notes. If I make a promise, I keep it.'

Kodai smiled at the notion. Some British idea of fair play, perhaps. 'When Radouk and I celebrate, our first toast will be to your probity, Cowley.' He appeared to enjoy the thought. 'Now – throw me the case.'

Cowley threw it – using every atom of strength – straight at Kodai's head. Then he started to run.

Calmly, Kodai dodged the case. Raising his gun, he took precise aim at the fleeing figure and fired three times, grouping the bullets with casual expertise. Cowley lurched, then spun as the bullets ripped into his body. His legs folded and he sprawled full-length in the sunlit mouth of the hangar.

Out on the perimeter, Bodie and Doyle heard the shots – and knew they could mean only one thing. They whirled round to see the figure of Kodai running towards the chopper. Instinctively, both men fired at the distant form, then sprinted towards the perimeter fence, hurdling it and firing again as Kodai hauled himself aboard. Their target was way out of range and they knew it, but they kept firing as they ran, watching the helicopter lift off, dip slightly, then clatter away gaining height and speed.

They pounded up to the hangar, breath rasping in their throats, then stopped. Inside, they could see Cowley's body stretched out on the hard-packed earth of the hanger floor. Slowly, almost in a daze, they approached it, neither speaking – barely able to take in the fact that the man was dead. Cowley – *dead*! In the dim, eerie light of the hangar, they stood over the corpse not knowing what to do, what to think.

'Was that you firing, Bodie?' the corpse asked tetchily. The partners looked at each other: shocked, delighted, angry – in that order. 'Come on,' growled their chief, 'help me up.' Grudgingly – and not too gently – they complied. '... And help me out of this thing,' he continued, removing his jacket to reveal the padded bulk of a 'second chance' bullet-proof waistcoat, which bore the impact marks of Kodai's slugs: three ragged tufts all within a couple of millimetres of each other and all over the heart. While they struggled with the waistcoat, Cowley repeated his question, making the most of the partners' confusion and his dramatic return from the dead: '*Was* it you, Bodie?'

Bodie holstered the offending weapon. 'Sir,' he said with an attempt at lightness, 'I cannot tell a lie.'

'Doyle?' No one was being let off the hook.

'Likewise, Sir,' admitted Doyle.

'I knew you would. Never could obey orders – either of you!' Leaving them there, Cowley strode out of the hangar into the sunshine.

Bodie recovered first. Pacing along behind, he said, 'Kodai could have killed you. What if he'd gone for a head shot?'

'At thirty yards, in a poor light – with a hand-gun?'

Cowley made it sound as if he'd taken no risk at all. He knew, though, that the whole thing had been a calculated gamble – he'd been pretty sure that Kodai wouldn't go in for any fancy shooting; and he'd been counting on the Russian's ability with a handgun – a wild shot could have proved fatal. But no one – not even George Cowley – could predict the unpredictable. This time, the gamble had paid off; but next time . . .

There was no time for that kind of speculation – no profit in it either; the game wasn't over yet. Cowley snapped out an order: 'Doyle, stand the men down, then come with me. And you, Bodie.'

Baffled, Doyle took out his pocket R/T and gave the instruction, then clambered into the car alongside Bodie, who was every bit as puzzled as his partner. 'Where are we going, Sir?' he asked.

'That remains to be seen,' replied Cowley mysteriously.

They crossed the airfield in a matter of seconds and Cowley swung the car out on to the narrow country road.

'Why aren't we taking the lads?' Doyle was still mystified.

'Because I don't want a bloody procession, Doyle.' Before any more questions could be asked, the car's R/T let out a torrent of completely unintelligible gobbledegook. Bodie's eyes widened. 'Nice friends you've got,' he smiled.

'Switch the scrambler in,' ordered his chief. Bodie snapped the switch and the garbled words took shape: 'John Brown calling Queen Vic . . . Come in please Queen Vic . . . John Brown . . .'

'I hear you John Brown,' answered Cowley. 'Please advise . . . Over!'

The disembodied, metallic voice cut in above a thin trickle of static. The Air Commodore's boys were really proving their worth: 'Target chopper heading three-one-five. Estimated speed 90 knots. Exact position now five-zero-five-zero north, zero-two-zero-one west . . . Over.'

'Thank you John Brown. Keep advising. Over.' Cowley replaced the R/T transmitter mike. 'Bodie, you're navigating.' He indicated a large-scale map on the dashboard. Picking it up, Bodie exchanged a glance with Doyle. Slowly, light was beginning to dawn!

They would have understood perfectly if they'd been able to see Radouk, standing on the lawn of a large country house some five miles away, peering at the sky through binoculars to catch the first glimpse of Kodai's helicopter. Everything had worked perfectly so far, but Radouk was apprehensive; he wouldn't feel happy until they were away clear. Going up against CI5 meant tackling the best agents and the best organisation in the world – it was foolish to take anything for granted.

'Target now five-zero-five-three north, zero-two-zero-four west. Heading steady: three one five . . .' The Air Force boys were well in control – feeding precise fixes on the helicopter's position to the CI5 car where Bodie was translating them into map references . . . though not without difficulty, as Cowley cornered at seventy, then pushed the vehicle to its limits on the hedge-lined back-roads.

'Take the next left, Sir.'

Following Bodie's instruction, Cowley asked, 'How far behind are we?'

'About five miles.'

Cowley accelerated out of the bend, banging his foot hard down to the accompaniment of a banshee wailing of rubber.

Radouk heard the chopper before he saw it; then his glasses picked it up coming in on a direct line and travelling fast. He smiled. The last act, he thought; the last act and a happy ending.

'Next right!' Bodie yelled. Cowley trod on the brake, wrenched the wheel over and slammed the throttle down as the rear of the car swept round in a controlled skid. The R/T cut in abruptly: 'John Brown to Queen Vic.

Chopper stationary at five-zero-five-north, zero-two-zero-four west. Losing altitude. Over.'

'Thank you John Brown.' Cowley knew that his prey had reached the lair. 'Please advise if chopper moves. Over.'

'Wilco, Queen Vic. Out.'

'This turn-off, Sir ...' Bodie's last syllable was drowned as his chief executed a perfect racing-change, drifted the car into the bend and boomed into the straight. Doyle reflected briefly that he couldn't have done it better himself.

Radouk approached the chopper as Kodai emerged from beneath the slowing rotor-blades. They faced each other.

'Well?' Radouk demanded.

Kodai smiled slowly and handed over the briefcase. 'A little bonus,' he joked.

'And Cowley?' – Radouk was eager to know.

Kodai's smile broadened as he drew his forefinger across his throat. Radouk was smiling now.

He might have been a lot less pleased had he seen Cowley's car travelling at an almost unthinkable speed some half a mile away. He might have made a quicker job of helping Kodai to push the helicopter out of sight beneath some trees – might have spent less time in getting his car out of the garage ... assuming he'd believed the evidence of his own eyes, of course. For Cowley was dead. Kodai had shot him – seen him go down. There was nothing to fear from Cowley ever again.

'It's got to be this place,' asserted Bodie, wrestling with the map,' Courtland House. The lawn's big enough for Concorde!'

Obediently, Cowley changed down and roared into the gravelled driveway of the country mansion – at the same moment as Radouk's car began to gather speed and head towards the road. The vehicles came at each other head-on. Cowley's face was set. He didn't lessen speed one jot – in fact he accelerated – and he kept the wheel completely steady. A deadly game of 'chicken'; and it was Radouk's nerve that snapped first. He yanked the wheel over hard, lost it on the loose gravel and slewed into a thick clump of bushes.

Cowley stood on the brakes and Bodie and Doyle were out of the car and moving. Radouk and Kodai had lost no time, either. Recovering quickly, they had used their few seconds advantage to find cover among the bushes. When Bodie made a move to get behind their position a bullet whipped past his head. Cowley and Doyle poured fire into the bushes to cover him.

Crouched in the undergrowth, Radouk and Kodai were both in a mild state of shock – not so much from the car crash as from the sight of Cowley – Cowley who had just driven a car straight at them, Cowley who was putting together the accurate string of shots that clipped leaves and twigs from nearby bushes ... Cowley very much alive!

'He's not even injured!' protested Radouk.

Kodai was incredulous. 'I shot him three times!' He shook his head as if to rid himself of an impossible vision. Radouk was quicker to accept the evidence of his eyes. 'I'll do a deal with you, Cowley,' he yelled. 'The name you want ... I'll still give it to you!'

Cowley's voice came back, loud and clear: 'I already know the name – and the man. I worked with him for twenty years.'

'Then why didn't you arrest him?' responded the Russian.

Cowley had been waiting for that question and he enjoyed providing the answer: 'Because he was working for us.' His voice contained more than a trace of glee. 'He was always working for us.'

The Russians looked at each other in horror. It couldn't be true! For twenty years, they'd been taking information from the man, acting on it, treating it always as top-priority. Their 'mole' in the highest ranks of British Intelligence had been one of the major coups in infiltrating the enemy camp. Whole strategies had been based on his dispatches. Cowley must be bluffing.

'I don't believe you Cowley!' bellowed Radouk. 'You don't know who the man is.'

'Keep him talking, Sir,' muttered Doyle urgently. He knew that Bodie would be working his way round to come up behind the two men. He just needed a few more seconds if Doyle's judgement was accurate.

'Was, Radouk!' Cowley shouted. 'Was! The man is dead.'

Radouk started with surprise. Then: 'You're bluffing Cowley!'

'I'm not. Freeze!' Bodie wasn't shouting: he didn't have to. His gun barrel was no more than six feet from Radouk's back. Obediently, Radouk froze. Kodai didn't. He spun round, his gun coming up fast – but not nearly fast enough. Bodie shot him twice in the chest, the twin explosions sounding almost as one. The Russian reared up, his arms and legs flailing awkwardly, then pitched over on his back. Radouk held his gun out where Bodie could see it, opened his fingers, and let the weapon fall beside his comrade's lifeless body. Then he stood up, to see Cowley and Doyle coming across the driveway.

For what seemed an age, Radouk and Cowley simply stared at one another; between them lay an antagonism too deep, too uncompromising for words. It was the Russian who spoke first: asking the question that lay at the heart of things – the question that showed he was beginning to understand the reasons for his defeat, the reasons for Cowley being one jump ahead for most of the time: 'How did you know about Meredith?'

Inwardly, Cowley smiled. Meredith! The joker in the pack – the one factor that should have given Radouk an overwhelming advantage but had proved, instead, to be the means of his downfall!

'I didn't,' Cowley replied, saving the best till last, '... until he said you'd spoken to our man at a time when I knew him to have been dead for a fortnight. I'd just been to his memorial service. Under the circumstances,' he went on wryly, as Radouk was ushered into the CI5 car, 'it was hardly surprising he couldn't help you!'

As Bodie and Doyle climbed in on either side of Radouk, they looked at each other and smiled. Just like Cowley to play his cards close to his chest. Now they understood – and could appreciate the perfect neatness of their chief's planning. Cowley wasn't relishing his moment of triumph, though. As he set the car in motion, he was recalling a dull day in a small churchyard and a fresh grave unmarked by any headstone. A man who had served his country ... a man who had to remain anonymous, even in death.

Chapter Six

The gun shop was an unimposing place: a small, shabby façade badly in need of a lick of paint, a low door with reinforced bars across the glass panel, a grimy window, webbed with steel-mesh, displaying a rack of guns and a few cartridge belts. It stood in a quiet London back-street: part of a terraced row that also housed a junk-store and a neighbourhood grocer's. There were no flashing signs, or neon representations of guns; nothing to advertise the place; but the experts knew of it – the gun club members, who spent their spare time hunkered down in the butts at the local rifle range, or the rough shooters, whose weekends were given over to tramping over the countryside with a twelve-bore in the crook of the arm and a pocket full of No. 6 cartridges. Others knew of it, too – experts in a deadlier game.

For the old man who owned the shop, it was the end of a long day. He shuffled over to the door and reversed the hanging sign so that it read 'Closed', then pottered back to the counter: just one last task before his work was done. He'd been oiling and cleaning his best gun – a gleaming Cogswell – and a large wrapping of greased paper was lying on the counter; this would protect the weapon from any grit or dust while it was in store.

The switching of the Open/Closed sign would have gone unnoticed save by someone who was actually watching for it. Across the road, waiting in a phone box, a man called Glover had been waiting for some minutes to spot just that tiny movement. He picked up the phone and began to dial.

With patient, precise movements, the old man folded the paper round the beautifully turned steel and smooth stock of the Cogswell. He was absorbed in the work; the shop was silent.

The explosion of noise, when it came, fixed him to the spot with shock. The lock splintered under a flat-footed kick and a tall figure, terrifying in a stocking mask that flattened his features grotesquely, cannoned through. The sawn-off shotgun he was carrying was pointed directly at the old man.

'Blink and you're dead!' The nylon mask did nothing to conceal the murderous tone. The shotgun stayed level as Glover, also wearing a stocking mask, came through the shattered door. The old man found his voice: 'No, please ... the till's there ... open ...'

'Wrong currency,' growled the gunman. Glover approached the gun racks and began to strip them, throwing the weapons into a sackcloth wrap he'd flung down on the floor.

'Those!' snapped the first man, indicating a row of chained guns and turning to the old man.

'Take everything ... everything ...' he fumbled with keys, eager to comply.

Soon, Glover had amassed a pile of rifles and shotguns. He hefted the bundle – a vast weight – and made to put them down again ... too many.

'The lot!' There was an edge of steel in the gunman's voice. 'We need every one we can get ... don't we?'

Glover's hesitation was only momentary. Obediently, he dragged the bundle to the door, opened it and looked out into the quiet street. The old man moved – as if for the open door.

'Don't do it!' The shotgun held him dead centre.

Glover shouldered the sack, pushed the door wider, and made for a Volkswagen van parked outside. The sight of freedom was too much for the old man. Pushing a chair towards his captor, he started a shambling run towards the street ... but he was never going to make it!

Doyle was cruising when the call came through: controlling the steering wheel with fingertip pressure, one elbow resting on the open car-window, the slipstream worrying his mop of curly hair. He was making for that very ordinary building in Whitehall that housed the very extraordinary Department CI5; but there was no hurry – he had the journey timed to the second.

'4/5 ... 4/5' – the R/T was so clear that the operator could have been sitting in the passenger seat. Doyle changed hands on the wheel and flicked the transmit button. 'Speak to me,' he murmured lazily.

'Alert. Dawkin's gun shop, Reynolds Avenue. Coded tip-off. Raid. Out.'

Doyle's attitude changed abruptly. He acknowledged the call with a curt: 'Roger!' then clapped his foot to the accelerator. The engine responded with a throaty roar. A coded tip-off: to Doyle that meant one of two things ... and both spelt trouble.

Glover and his sidekick – Duffy – had peeled off the stocking masks as they leapt into the waiting Volkswagen van. Duffy took the wheel, careful to keep the van down to a legal speed, and after five minutes or so pulled up outside a row of private garages only half a dozen streets away. Glover got out and hauled at one of the doors – a double garage that housed an anonymous looking, ten-year-old Cortina. As Duffy edged the van into the garage, Glover was reversing the car into the street. The switch took no more than a minute. With Duffy beside him now, Glover swung the car round and headed back towards Reynolds Avenue.

In the same instant that Doyle's car rocked to a halt outside the gun shop, a squad car roared in from the opposite end of the street. Doyle saw it, but didn't wait for the support team – he was out and running. The two plain-clothes men who had also answered the alert raced into the shop behind him.

The old man lay on the floor, groaning, the blood

from a head-wound matting his hair. Doyle took in the scattered weapons, the empty racks; he pointed to the back of the shop. 'Check it,' he ordered. One of the plain-clothes men moved swiftly behind the counter. From outside came a squeal of tyres and the sound of a car door slamming. Doyle stepped out on to the pavement as Bodie arrived on the scene.

Seventy yards away, Glover and Duffy sat in the parked Cortina and watched. They'd picked a spot that gave them a full view of the gun shop, knowing that no one would expect the thieves to be that close. Between the cars and the smashed shop-door, the figures of the two agents could be seen: Bodie listening intently as Doyle briefed him. Duffy's eyes were fixed on Doyle's face; he neither blinked, nor switched his gaze; his mouth was drawn into a thin line of maniacal hatred.

'That's Doyle,' he said at last, spitting the name out as if it had a foul taste. 'That's our man!'

George Cowley hefted the twelve-bore pump-action shotgun and sighted for a moment down the barrel. He'd arrived in time to see the shop-owner taken off to hospital. Now he was eager to get on with the job of checking exactly what had been taken. Beside him Doyle was flicking through a stock-record book. Cowley laid the gun down alongside ten or so others that remained.

'Elephant-stoppers,' he observed worriedly. 'Hardly the stuff for the local Cadet Corps. I thought there was supposed to be a limit on stocking these things.'

'There is,' Doyle agreed, not looking up from the sheets of the ledger.

Bodie had been doing some checking of his own. Now he came in looking tense and angry. 'The call was coded: came through to C-11 at the Yard in the usual way.' There was something ominous in his words and Cowley detected it.

'It must have been someone who knows the Organisation's tactics,' he replied warily.

Bodie was much more positive: 'They're moving forces again.'

'Maybe.' Cowley was still cautious.

'Obviously!' Bodie was in no doubt.

'*Maybe*,' rapped Cowley. Bodie matched his chief's glare with a fierce look of his own. 'We've been fighting wars with the Organisation long enough to learn to read the signs.'

'All right,' Cowley's look was still hostile, 'there's a gun robbery; all right – someone uses their tip-off code. But that's not enough. There's no reason *why* they would be operative now.'

Bodie felt that the evidence spoke for itself. 'If it's not them ... ?' he didn't bother to finish, just looked down at Doyle who had completed his work with the stock-ledger.

'Six shots,' offered Doyle, 'eight twenty-twos, four Parker Hales.'

Bodie sounded victorious: 'That's not pawn-shop traffic. This was a pro job. These guys wanted guns for an armoury and they knew where to come.'

'Then why didn't they take the lot?' Cowley wanted to know.

'Maybe they were disturbed,' Doyle offered.

'Eye witnesses?' countered his chief. Doyle shook his head, accepting the point. Bodie was in a mood to accept nothing, though. He confronted Cowley. 'We've been through this sort of run enough times to know when the Organisation's at it. Everything fits. Exactly their style. Even the tip-off – dissent in the ranks. We've had that fifty times before.'

'But not in the last year,' argued Cowley. 'Why now?'

Bodie wasn't listening; he was heated, looking for action. 'If this does mean they're active again, what do we do? Sit around till someone's blown to Kingdom Come?'

'No!' Cowley knew they had to find the truth. 'Go

and prove it. Find out if this *is* the start of a campaign.' It was all Bodie needed; he started for the door before his chief had finished speaking. 'But . . .' added Cowley sharply '. . . step on anyone's toes and next week you're pen-pushing.' He moved closer to Bodie and spoke in a tone that made it clear he would stand for no wildcat action. 'There's a festering bubble out there . . . and it's just waiting to burst.'

Cowley's fears had nothing to do with timidity. He was as keen as the next man to come to grips with the vicious network of organised crime that had declared open war on society and kept CI5 ignominiously on the hop. The Organisation! Cowley had directed many operations against the men who ran it – men who would use guns, torture, the dirtiest methods without a second thought; rich men, who lived outside the law, whose very existence was a challenge to Cowley. He'd won battles, often, but he hadn't come close to winning the war. The Organisation's tentacles reached everywhere; and as soon as one was lopped off, another seemed to grow in its place.

No, Cowley wasn't one to retreat from that particular fight. But he knew that, for the present, the Organisation had seen fit to play things quietly – and the last thing George Cowley wanted to do was fire the first bullet in a shooting war. His job was to protect innocent citizens, not involve them in a cross-fire! He had to agree with Bodie, though, that the gun shop job looked a lot like Organisation work. Were they taking a rest – or simply biding their time?

Cowley's confusion would have been greater had he been able to see, later the same day, the Volkswagen van with the guns bouncing and rattling in the back, trundling in reverse along a narrow riverside path some forty miles west of London. Duffys brought the vehicle to a halt with the rear wheels almost overhanging the bank, so that the doors would open directly above the sluggish, dark flow of the river. Glover hopped out of the passenger seat and ran round to open the double doors at the back. The guns slid down the metal floor of the van and spilled out into the water.

Glover watched them sink, then he turned to give Duffy the okay and in that moment caught a glimpse of a car coming to a stop on the road above them. A girl and a man got out and started to make their way downhill towards the river-bank. Duffy had been careful to pick a secluded spot to dump the guns – it hadn't occurred to him that a place like that would be a lovers' Paradise.

'Come on! There's someone coming!' Glover virtually screamed the words as he hurled himself back into the van. Duffy turned the key. The engine churned but wouldn't fire. The lovers had noticed nothing as yet – wrapped up in a private world; but they were getting closer. Duffy tried again. The engine fired and he let the clutch in with a bang. The wheels spun frantically in the mud of the river bank.

'That's all we need,' babbled Glover. 'Get seen here and that's it, end of the game.'

'Shut up!' Duffy was concentrating on his skidding rear wheels – trying to ease the clutch in and find a purchase on the mud.

'What's wrong? What is it?' Glover was frantic.

'Come on you ... Go ... !' Duffy cursed the van as it rocked and lurched at the water's edge; then one wheel found a rough patch of earth and the vehicle slewed, then started to travel along the track. On the other side of a small screen of trees, the lovers glanced up incuriously and watched it go, pleased that they would now have the place to themselves.

Chapter Seven

Ray Doyle had woken up knowing that there was something unpleasant in store for him. For an instant, he couldn't remember what – then it came back. Call on Morgan. It would be an edgy business. Morgan had left the department under a cloud; in fact, he'd been kicked out. A mistake had been made and Cowley had put it down to Morgan. There was no appeal under those circumstances: Cowley was judge, jury and executioner. He never apologised and never explained. It made for long-lived resentments.

The department kept tabs on 'old boys'; Doyle knew exactly where to find his ex-colleague. He rapped on the door of the poky flat and had to wait for a couple of minutes before Morgan answered, clad in nothing but a pair of jeans. Clearly, he'd just got out of bed.

Seeing Doyle, he sneered, 'Not today, mate,' and made to close the door. Doyle wedged his foot into the gap. 'C'mon, Morgan. We're old pals. I'm not flying the flag.'

Reluctantly, Morgan allowed him to push into the flat: just in time to be treated to the sight of Morgan's girlfriend, Sylvie, scrambling naked out of the tousled bed and dragging a sheet round her body. 'Nothing sacred anymore?' she spat, glaring at Doyle. Morgan seemed unmoved. 'Go on,' he told her, 'see if that coffee's ready.'

As she went through to the kitchen, Doyle observed: 'Must be doing well if you can afford an au pair.'

Morgan was struggling into a shirt. 'No,' he countered sourly, 'you've got the wrong end of it. All this free time's one of the perks of not being employed. Know what I mean?'

Doyle attempted a smile. 'Plenty of time to think, eh?'

'I spend most of my time forgetting!'

'Don't blame you.' Doyle tried to take some of the heat out of the exchange. 'I'd do the same.'

Morgan faced him squarely. 'What does that mean?'

'Like I said ... If I got a rap on the knuckles for something I didn't do, I'd spend most of my time trying not to feel sorry for myself.'

Morgan gazed at Doyle thoughtfully for a while, trying to read his expression. Eventually he asked: 'What do you want?

'Question and answer time?' Doyle tried to make it sound like a parlour game.

'I'm not on the payroll any more,' snapped Morgan as Sylvie, who had found some clothes by this time, returned and made her way to a drinks table in the corner of the room.

'Coffee's up,' she announced. 'I'll settle for a drink, if you don't mind ...'

Doyle ignored her. 'Gun robbery,' he said, looking at Morgan. The girl started at the words. 'Go feed the cat, Sylvie.' Morgan wasn't hinting, he was ordering. She shrugged and went back to the kitchen as Morgan crossed over to the drinks table and poured himself a slug of neat Scotch. 'Ironic,' he continued, '... two years ago I was everyone's darling because my wife's people had connections with the Organisation. Then Cowley puts me in as a sleeper. I'm risking life and limb ... everything goes wrong ... I'm left carrying the can.'

'Someone blew the whistle on us and a man got killed,' Doyle reminded him. 'You were the only common denominator.'

Morgan rounded on him. 'You think I got drunk and talked!'

'No. But put yourself in Cowley's shoes ...'

The other man laughed bitterly and downed his drink. 'So, having been dishonourably discharged ...' he paused for effect, 'CI5 would like some information about the Organisation's activities?'

'Yeah.' Doyle was smiling, but he knew there was little enough to laugh at; he hated using Morgan this way.

'Well,' came the response, 'number one – I don't have the connections I used to have ... not even the wife I used to have. And number two – if I knew the old crowd were planning the third world war, I wouldn't give it to you.'

'You working?' Doyle tried a different tack, and the question surprised Morgan for a moment.

'Bit of lorry-driving,' he answered honestly. 'Odds and ends.'

Doyle took a note out of his pocket and put it on the bedside table. 'I owe you a tenner. That Christmas poker session.' Morgan smiled at the lie, but took no offence. He believed Doyle was genuinely sympathetic; and he wasn't about to say 'no' to the money. In a way it amused him to watch the CI5 man's discomfort. Before he could comment, Sylvie returned, dressed and made-up to go out. 'I can't stay here forever' – this to Doyle as much as to Morgan, 'I've got a job to get back to.'

Doyle registered the hint and made for the door, pausing just long enough to rattle off some information: 'Gun shop raid. Shotguns and two-twos ... with a coded tip-off.' Morgan's expression gave nothing away. 'Thanks for the coffee –' Doyle didn't wait for a response.

Morgan stared after him as Sylvie gathered a few possessions from the bedside table and stuffed them into her bag, chattering as she did so. 'I doubt if I'll see you tonight. I'll probably do the late shift at the club ...' She stopped, then asked in a more serious voice: 'What was all that about gun shops?'

'They think a terrorist campaign's brewing,' Morgan answered levelly.

'Oh?' Her face showed nothing; she watched Morgan idly twisting Doyle's tenner in his fingers.

'You could find out at the club,' he said casually.

She kissed her fingertips and pressed them to his lips.

'You're not a copper any more,' she said lightly, 'and there's a certain kind of client I don't mix with.'

Morgan pushed the bank note into her breast pocket with slow deliberation. 'Keep your ear to the ground,' he said.

Ted and Davis were hard men: not wantonly violent, not wild – but hard. And they were a team; people knew that, just as they knew that the older one was always known by his Christian name and the younger was just 'Davis'. As a team, they'd seen plenty of trouble and they knew how to cope. In fact, the trouble was usually of their making; after all, it was their job.

They'd been watching the row of suburban houses for some time – Davis sitting in the car and staring fixedly down the street, watching the movements of residents and passers by, while Ted took off now and then to scout the neighbourhood. He'd left, a few minutes earlier, to make a phone call from a nearby call-box when they'd spotted their mark – Glover – returning from a shopping expedition.

Glover was unpacking his groceries when the phone rang. He turned down a blaring radio and lifted the instrument cautiously, as if it might blow up in his hand.

'Hello!' There was silence. 'Hello? Who is it? Hello!' The line went dead as Ted replaced his receiver and went back to the car. 'Only Glover,' he informed Davis. 'You sure there's been no movement?'

'I've been four hours here,' came the reply. 'Some old geezer came out to tinker with his car. Two tasty-looking ladies did their daily shopping – and Glover did his. That's it.'

'Duffy's in there,' growled Ted. 'I'd stake my life on it.' He pondered for a moment, then came to a decision. 'Come on – we'll try it.'

They crossed to the building that housed Duffy's flat, Davis moving down a side entrance to cover the back, while Ted went up a flight of stairs to the front door.

He knocked and heard Glover's voice answer immediately. 'Yes?'

'Gas meter.' Odd – it was an old trick, but somehow people always opened the door to the gas man; he was taken on trust, like the doctor who told you to take foul-tasting medicine. As the door came open a fraction, Ted smashed his shoulder into it, following through into the room and pinning Glover against a wall before he'd had time to recover. 'What the hell ... ?' was all he had time for before Ted's gun was wedged into his belly.

'Never trust gas meter men,' he rasped, twisting the barrel of the revolver slightly so Glover could really feel it. 'Now then ... where's Duffy?'

'Who? What are you talking about?' Glover blustered.

'Play games and you're dead. Duffy's with you. He's been seen.'

'Not with me!'

'Silly to try that, sonny.' Ted's free hand closed round Glover's throat, fingers and thumb gouging into the flesh. '... 'Cause you've been seen – both of you. Now, what happened? Split in the ranks up north was it? So Duffy decided to try the big city, eh?' The fingers tightened and Glover's face contorted with pain. 'Where is he?'

'Cal ... Calais.' Glover choked the word out, then slumped back against the wall as Ted released him.

'Why Calais?' The gun was still levelled.

'He ... he said he was fed up here ... wanted to get away.' Glover's words came painfully.

'You're sure that's not just a little bedtime story?' Ted was menacing.

'Swear it!'

'Then who did the gun robbery?'

'Don't know what you're talking about,' Glover protested. Ted considered this, then held the gun up to the other man's face, twisting it in the light, before slipping it into his shoulder holster. 'Calais is the best place for Duffy,' he said slowly, 'since Mr Albie is interested in him.' He watched Glover's reaction to the name and knew that he'd made his point. 'Maybe you should join him ... in Calais.'

Across the stairway, Duffy watched through the hair-line crack of a door-jamb as Ted went back down the stairs to the street. He waited until he heard the outside door slam, and only then did he take his hand away from the mouth of the terrified young housewife whose flat he'd invaded. The mysterious phone call had been enough to send him scurrying for cover – just in case; and his suspicions had been justified. When in doubt, assume the worst – it was a practice that had kept Duffy healthy many times before. Never trust gas meter men, and never trust to luck.

The girl was shaking with fear, scarcely able to comprehend what was happening to her. Callously, Duffy threw her down on to a sofa, ripped the belt from her dress and made a hurried job of tying her hands and binding her mouth with a handkerchief. Then he crossed the hall into his own flat and grabbed a holdall from the bedroom.

'Albie's looking for you,' whimpered Glover as Duffy packed. 'They must know.'

Duffy didn't look up from his task. 'Just let's get out of here,' he mouthed, '– all right?'

Bodie looked up disinterestedly as the blue van flashed its headlights then pulled into the kerb. He didn't need back-up, he figured, to take this load of jokers across the road. He glanced away from the support car towards the peeling paint of the building opposite. DRINKWELL & SON, TURF ACCOUNTANT had been painted over with FRONT PAGE BETTING OFFICE. May as well be now as later, he thought, and turned to the man in the passenger seat: a heavy from A-Squad. 'Right,' he said, 'let's flex our muscles.'

As he climbed out of the car, four men from the van came across to join him. They went into the betting shop fast, Bodie carrying his ·38 Smith & Wesson; as he'd guessed, there wasn't much opposition. Two girls – clerks – stood behind the counter alongside a shabby-looking individual who was checking receipts. Two punters were scrutinising the card for the next meeting. Otherwise, the place was showing little sign of life. At the sight of Bodie's gun, one of the girls screamed; the sound clashed with Bodie's command: 'All right. The shop's closed!'

There was a moment's uncertainty from the character behind the counter, then he flung himself across Bodie's line of fire to get to a door leading to the back of the shop, crashed through it and was gone. In almost the same instant, a second man appeared from the back, looking puzzled at first, then freezing as one of the Squad men produced a gun. 'Shut off the back!' Bodie yelled, then vaulted the counter and pounded after the runaway.

The laneways behind the shop were like a maze, but Bodie spotted his man leaping a fence at the end of a blind alley. The agent had made after him, gaining about ten yards in thirty and realising instantly that his quarry wasn't fit enough to make much of a chase of it. They bowled through a series of tatty gardens and backyards with Bodie closing all the time, until the fleeing figure put on a final, desperate burst of speed and disappeared round a corner by some restaurant back-entrances.

When Bodie arrived at the same spot, he stopped – knowing full well that the man hadn't made enough of a break to be out of sight. He looked around at the piles of crates and sacks of slippery garbage, then his eyes travelled to a large bin. Hefting a crate, Bodie trotted forward and lobbed it into the top. Immediately there was an agonised cry from the depths of the bin. Bodie threw his weight against the rough tin, smashing the receptacle to the ground. The fugitive rolled out, holding a face that had been bloodied by the rough slats of the crate. Amused, Bodie hauled him out of the slushy rubbish of food remnants. 'Going to roost in your natural habitat, Philo?' he asked.

Back in the betting shop, the humour in Bodie's voice changed to a sweet reasonableness. Philo and the other man – Davis – sat sullenly while Bodie spoke: 'I'm not asking for names and addresses,' he assured them, 'just strategic movements. Why is the Organisation active again?' There was no response. 'Right then.' Bodie began to sound less reasonable. 'Step two – we separate the love-birds,' he pulled both men to their feet and beckoned a squad man over, 'and see who starts singing first.'

At that moment, Cowley and Doyle arrived: Cowley leading and looking savagely angry. Davis addressed A-Squad's chief at once. 'This kind of victimisation is against the law. You won't get away with this.' There was fury in his voice as well as fear; a squad man led them both away and Cowley turned on Bodie. 'Let them go. *Now!*'

'I was just beginning,' Bodie protested.

'Are you mad?' Cowley's face was rigid with anger. 'Half a dozen armed men crashing into a shop in broad daylight to pull in two toy-town bandits!'

'Philo and Davis,' Bodie emphasised. 'They're top boys in the Organisation. Philo did eighteen months for possession . . .'

'Six years ago,' broke in Cowley. 'Look, I warned you. Stir them up, get the old boys going, and we'll have a major war on our hands. And this,' he gestured round at the shop, the armed squad men, 'is just the kind of bravado that'll start it!'

'So what do we do?' Bodie was angry, too. 'Advertise in the papers?'

'No,' came the icy response. 'You use your head Bodie – like Doyle!' On that note, Cowley stormed out, leaving Bodie in a seething rage. He turned to his partner, fists clenched. 'Well, professor?' he demanded.

Doyle ran a hand through his tangled curls. 'We know where they drink, don't we?'

Bodie was scornful. 'That's the alternative, is it?' he sneered. 'Go around drinking in the back-street pubs?' Doyle didn't bother to reply, but he countered Bodie's hard look with one of his own.

It wasn't a back-street pub – more a sort of alleyway dive, a place where you could get almost anything you wanted ... even a drink, provided you were prepared to pay the prices they asked. The dedicated boozer could drink a beer at champagne prices, or champagne at unthinkable prices; the lonely could find expensive company; and villains could meet and talk in relative privacy.

The place was bathed in a dim, orange light and, since it was early, you didn't have to part curtains of smoke to look at the person next to you. Bodie occupied a stool at the bar and waited till the barmaid turned to take his order. Sylvie – her make-up leaving her face older, more shop-worn.

'What can I order that's potent and legal?' Bodie smiled.

'You ask and I'll see if I can oblige.' It was said as a challenge to the double-meaning in his question. Bodie smiled again, less wolfishly this time. 'Lemonade,' he said, 'care to join me?'

'I'm boss here tonight,' she said, 'so it's work, not pleasure.'

'Lemonade won't take you too high,' he retorted. Sylvie reached down a glass and began to unscrew the top from a lemonade bottle. Before she could pour, Bodie pointed behind her to a Vodka bottle on the shelf. 'With a little of that.' She smiled this time ... and added the liquor. 'Who are the villains round here?' asked Bodie casually, taking the drink. 'You being the boss – you'd know.'

'What are you?' she teased, 'the village bobby?'

'No. I want someone to fill in my accountant!' Sylvie

laughed and Bodie used the moment to gain some ground. 'Last time I was here,' he said, 'there was a police raid . . .'

'Oh?' she seemed genuinely intrigued. 'Club wasn't licensed?'

'Something like that,' said Bodie, still advancing. Then – 'Who are the tough men here?'

Sylvie stonewalled him. 'Ask me about the girls and I might be able to tell you.' Then she moved off, adding, 'Enjoy your drink.' Moodily, Bodie watched her go.

He might have brightened somewhat if he'd been able to see four newcomers to the club who were being shown to a secluded alcove table . . . or, more accurately, he'd have been interested in the two men. The women, one a brassy bottle blonde, the other a well-endowed brunette, seated themselves at the table while their escorts – Ted and his boss, Mr Albie, had a muttered conversation with the doorman. Albie was leaning forward slightly to catch what the doorman was saying. He was a neatly dressed man, pushing middle-age and with a deceptively mild set to his features. All in all, he looked a lot like a bank manager or a moderately successful businessman; no-one who knew him, though, was fooled by the appearance. Albie was rough, tough and ruthless.

'. . . I think Sylvie would be the best one to help you,' the doorman was saying. He turned to beckon the girl over and, when she arrived, said, 'Sylvie, Mr Albie and his friends are looking for somebody. See if you can help.'

Albie took out a wallet and extracted a photograph of Duffy, handing it to Sylvie. 'Has he been around?'

She paused a second; then – 'I don't recognise him. I usually remember new faces, but we've been so understaffed . . .'

Ted's tone was less mild than Albie's. 'We were told he was here.'

'Well, maybe he was,' Sylvie replied lightly. 'Maybe one of the other girls saw him.'

'You're captain of the ship at the moment?' Albie's question. Sylvie nodded. 'Good girl,' he was turning on the charm. 'Don't envy you. Look –' he took his card and a five pound note from the wallet, '– this is pretty important. If you do see him – that's where you can get me . . .' she took the card, '. . . and that's for your trouble.' Sylvie hesitated, then took the money and moved off.

'Waste of time,' observed Ted.

Albie's tone had none of the softness he'd used for Sylvie. 'Sooner or later, he'll show at Glover's. You just keep a watch on it.'

As they made their way over to join their women, Sylvie was taking a tray of drinks to an upstairs room where a card game was in progress. Duffy was feeling pretty good: he'd won the last three pots and was sitting on a full house of Jacks and tens. Sylvie watched a couple of rounds of betting, then sidled over to him, collecting empty glasses as she went. 'Someone's looking for you,' she said quietly.

Duffy looked up, but didn't recognise the face; he liked what he saw though. 'Really?' She offered nothing more so he asked, 'Where?'

'Downstairs.' She moved away, needing to say no more, and as she did so her eyes fixed on Duffy's. There was fire in the look: mutual fire. Duffy got up and handed his winning cards to Glover. 'Play my hand for a minute,' he said and moved over to join Sylvie, out of earshot of the other players. 'Friend is he . . . ?'

'Maybe.' She looked up and again the spark was there between them. 'Mr Albie. You know him?'

There was a flicker of fear, now, diluting the open desire in Duffy's eyes. 'You tell him I was here?' She didn't reply. 'He show you a photo?' Duffy persisted.

'We see nothing and hear nothing,' she reassured him. 'That's the policy in here.'

'You told him you didn't see me?' Her silence told him that she had. 'That's very generous of you.'

'If you're in some sort of trouble,' she warned, 'it's

not very safe. Some of the other girls might say they've seen you.'

'No, I'm not in any trouble.' The lie came naturally. 'But I'd rather stay away from Albie ... He's probably recruiting.'

'I wouldn't know.'

Duffy tried a different approach: 'I suppose you get a fair few Squad people around here – plenty of narks?' She moved towards the door, unspeaking. Before she could reach it, he continued, 'How about a drink?'

'Here?' – genuine surprise in her voice.

'Why not,' said Duffy, his charm working overtime, 'I always believed in living dangerously.' His smile widened as she came back to join him.

Downstairs, Albie and Ted were settling themselves at the alcove table, when Ted spotted someone he *didn't* want to see; he nudged Albie and pointed to where Bodie sat at the bar chatting to a waitress whose IQ was probably smaller than her bust measurement. 'Bodie, CI5.' Ted's mouth twisted. 'He pulled Davis and Philo.'

Albie sighed in an exaggerated manner: rather as if he'd witnessed a display of bad manners at a dinner party. 'On Organisation territory?' he asked, shaking his head reprovingly.

'We can't have them living on our doorstep,' Ted exclaimed.

Albie watched Bodie chatting brightly. 'CI5 know the rules,' – it was spoken unemotionally, as if the agent had been caught cheating at Scrabble. 'He hit Davis. We hit him!'

Chapter Eight

'Section Six. Call for Bodie. Coded prefix.' Bodie was feeling some slight effect from his drinking session at the club the previous evening, which is why Doyle was at the wheel of their car, weaving skilfully through light traffic as they left the Whitehall office. Bodie had the window down on the passenger's side and was attempting to get some fresh air to his throbbing brow. A thin miasma of exhaust fumes washed over him, providing no relief at all.

'Yeah . . .' was all he said to the R/T operator; lacking any better instruction, she switched the caller through and Davis's voice was heard: 'Bodie?'

'I'm listening.'

'We want a meet. Ridge Farm. You know it?'

'Yeah. When?' Bodie definitely wasn't in a chatty mood.

'Half an hour,' – an equally curt reply from Davis before he hung up. Bodie replaced the transceiver and looked over at Doyle, who asked: 'One of our toytown bandits?'

Cowley's remark still rankled with Bodie. 'Alpha plus, professor,' he said chippily. Doyle decided not to enter the contest; instead, he changed down and swung the wheel to make a U-turn.

Ridge Farm had once been a thriving stud farm. Now there was nothing left but a few rows of stables and loose-boxes in bad repair surrounded by an acre or so of overgrown ground that had been used as a dumping ground for unwanted baths, malfunctioning stoves and threadbare items of furniture. The partners rounded the line of stables to see Davis's car parked face-on towards them. They parked nose-to-nose with it, then climbed out and looked carefully round. 'Nice rendezvous,' observed Bodie. 'Plenty of cover.'

'They wouldn't dare!' scoffed Doyle. As he spoke, a man stepped into view a hundred yards or so away. It was Ted, standing with his hands in his pockets, unspeaking, and making no move towards the CI5 men. 'That means "Come to Mummy", doesn't it?' joked Bodie. He and Doyle began to walk across the rubble-strewn ground.

'There's two of them.' Ted was talking to Albie, who stood just out of sight behind the stable-end.

'That's all right,' came the calm reply, 'Davis can take 'em both.'

Davis knew that too; he also knew who he was going to take first! The cross-hairs on the telescopic sight of his rifle pinpointed the bridge of Bodie's nose, slid down across his heart, wavered almost reluctantly for a second, then settled on his right knee-cap. It was the cruellest way ... to spare the man's life only to condemn him to a future of pain and uselessness. For a man like Bodie to be crippled would be worse than being killed outright – and Davis knew it.

'Come on,' Bodie shouted to Ted, 'we didn't bring the posse. Let's talk.'

Yes, Bodie first, though Davis. He held his breath to steady the cross-hairs, took the first millimetre of slack out of the trigger, then squeezed – just as Bodie stumbled slightly on the mound of earth and brick rubble he was crossing. He toppled forward, saving himself from falling full length with an outstretched hand in the same moment that Davis's shot thunked harmlessly into the ground behind him. The gunflash gave away Davis's rooftop position. As Bodie curled and rolled for safety behind the mound of debris, Doyle yanked out his Browning and pumped a few quick shots towards the rifleman's perch, then swung round to loose a couple off at Ted who was already drawing a bead on the agents. Ted skipped quickly sideways to join Albie under cover. As Doyle made to go after him, more shots came from the rifle, pinning him down. When he next raised his head, Davis had gone – sliding hurriedly down behind the row of stables and running in a wide arc towards the farm gate.

Doyle started after him, then stopped and turned as he heard the sound of Davis's car starting. Bodie heard it too, aiming a shot as the vehicle slammed past their own car, then bumped crazily over the rough track to intercept the line of Davis's run. Brakes screeched as the car slowed almost to a halt; then Davis was inside and hauling on the half-closed door.

The agents sprinted to their own car, but pulled up disappointedly as they got close. Davis's car had rammed the front wheels into a row of jagged slates. Air whistled from one of the tyres.

'Davis!' observed Bodie as he holstered his gun. He was about to go on, when the R/T crackled: *3.7? 3.7?* – Cowley's voice.

'3.7' acknowledged Bodie.

'Those guns the Organisation stole for the war you're convinced has started ...'

'What about them?'

'They've been found,' said Cowley, wishing he could be there to see the looks on the faces of his two operatives,' – at the bottom of a river!'

Bodie and Doyle arrived as a frogman was retrieving the last few weapons. Cowley was watching intently as the partners came up to him – Doyle walking past to check a few points with the frogman. 'Young couple saw the van,' Cowley informed Bodie. 'Then they read about the raid – and read the descriptions. Dumped! Hardly looks like stock-piling for an armoury, does it?'

Bodie didn't bother to acknowledge the obvious; instead he tried an attack: 'Davis ... that toytown bandit you unleashed on an unsuspecting public yesterday – he just tried to rearrange my physique with an Armalite!' He tapped his knee meaningfully.

'Tit-for-tat,' said Cowley unemotionally. 'You get Davis; Davis tries to blow your knee-cap. The story goes on. And on. And we learn nothing.'

Bodie disagreed. 'We know it *is* some kind of active campaign,' he insisted. Doyle returned before Cowley could comment. 'That's about it,' he gestured back towards the pile of guns on the river bank. 'All accounted for, minus one. They'll keep checking the river.'

'And were they dumped directly after the raid?' Bodie wanted to know.

'Looks like it.'

Cowley was puzzled. 'Makes no sense,' he said, 'unless someone's playing a game ... and making dirt for the Organisation.'

'Like who?' Bodie asked.

Doyle supplied an answer: 'Like a runner. Result of a split within the Organisation.' Cowley looked at him sharply. A runner ...

Glover's car moved slowly down a north London backstreet until it came to the small double gate of a repair-garage. The tyres crunched over debris as Glover drove into the yard, past the shells of a couple of beaten-up motors and pulled up in front of two men who were chewing on their lunch-time sandwiches. The taller of the two, Harry, was admiring the truly amazing proportion of the gate-fold girl in his soft-porn magazine.

'Guy called Harry?' enquired Glover.

Harry dragged his eyes away from the sprawled blonde and transferred his gaze to Glover's Cortina. 'We're booked up,' he said.

'After hours work,' offered Glover; both men suddenly looked more interested. 'I was told you're strongly recommended.'

Harry eyed him, rising interest tempered by caution. 'Depends on the offer,' he said warily.

*

Sitting in the club some time later, Glover felt satisfied with the business he'd done with Harry. Smiling, he raised his glass to Duffy who sat at the table with him, and to Sylvie who was beside Duffy and dressed in her 'off duty' clothes. The club was quiet – the lunchtime rush over – and a few people were downing the last brandy over the remains of their lunches.

Sylvie didn't see Morgan enter the club – didn't see him collect a beer from the bar, scan the room then start towards her. She didn't see him until he was standing over her, looking menacing and angry. 'Oh – you! I didn't think . . .' Her words came jumbled by astonishment. Morgan looked away from her towards Duffy as he said: 'Not expecting me, were you?'

'I forgot about lunch. This is . . .' she gestured weakly.

'Jack,' Duffy filled in the name and put out a hand to take Morgan's. Then he nodded at Glover: 'This is Steve.' Morgan nodded an acknowledgement as Duffy rose to leave, nudging Glover. 'Sylvie's been telling us all the native gossip,' continued Duffy.

'New around here, are you?' asked Morgan tightly.

'Not natives,' grinned Duffy. Then – 'Well . . . Be seeing you.'

'You won't stay for another drink?' There was a plea in Sylvie's invitation.

'Thanks anyway . . . See you,' said Duffy and left with Glover in tow. Morgan occupied the chair Duffy had just left. He took a swig of his beer, then asked: 'Who's he?'

Sylvie tried to keep her voice level. 'Didn't I tell you about him? Fellow I met a few nights ago.' Seeing Morgan's frown, she expanded the information: 'Involved with the Organisation . . . or something.'

Morgan watched her face. 'They're active at the moment, are they?' he demanded. And when she made no reply, his look hardened, though his tone remained casual. 'Well, come on . . . I'm just asking if you know.'

'Yes,' she admitted, 'he said they were. There's a robbery being set up. A gaming club ... which is neither your nor my business – right?' He nodded, which gave her some incentive to continue: 'Anyway, whatever they're up to, this place is boiling over with question-and-answer men just now.'

Morgan laughed dryly, enjoying a private joke. 'Poor Doyle,' he chuckled, '– on his hands and knees for a break.'

Sylvie looked startled at the mention of the CI5 man. 'Yeah – well, you keep your nose out of it.' There was fear in her voice, but concern as well. Morgan detected it. 'And you avoid that nark,' he said, offering a warning of his own.

The porno-mag lay next to the greaseproof-wrapped sandwiches on Harry's workbench, waiting for the mid-day break. Harry's routine didn't vary much – except when there was a special job to be done; a job like the one he was discussing with Glover on the phone.

'We know the layout,' he was saying, 'and we know the cash'll be there. The manager sleeps on the premises.'

Glover wanted to make sure the details were understood. 'We'll give you covering fire,' he said, '... if it comes to it.'

'Where from?' Harry didn't want to catch a stray bullet.

'Never mind. Trust me. You're dead safe. It's the easiest twenty per cent you'll ever earn.'

Harry wasn't too happy at being kept in the dark. 'Are we allowed to ask who this cash is to be donated to?' he asked sarcastically.

'Funny!' But Glover wasn't amused. 'Just deliver it as arranged.' He hung up and left the phone box to join Duffy on the pavement. 'Great!' – Duffy was full of gleeful anticipation. 'They're all set?' When Glover nodded, he continued, 'Well – let's get moving. You get out on the scene – keep an eye on them. But keep safe.'

As they got into the waiting car, his delight was evident. 'This one'll set both sides on fire – eh?' There was something unsettling, something crazy, in his full-blooded roar of laughter.

Chapter Nine

The girl slept without moving, one knee drawn up, one slender arm thrown across the pillow to frame a face that was as beautiful in sleep as when she was awake. A black torrent of hair flowed down her naked back, glossily reflecting the light as Bodie stirred and rolled over in his sleep, disturbing the covers.

Doyle stood in the twilight of the curtained room watching them breathe in unison; then he took a shirt from a chairback and threw it – with unnecessary force – at the smug expression of Bodie's sleeping face. Bodie came to, clawing the shirt away, and looked up.

'Tip-off,' Doyle informed him.

The girl stirred as Bodie clambered out of bed and began to struggle into the shirt. 'At nine a.m.,' he groused, '– it's obscene!'

Doyle gazed down at the girl as she began to waken. Then he put something on the pillow next to her face: 'You ought to be more careful ... Your latch-key.' She regarded him through a haze of sleep and warm, dreamy comfort. 'Good night?' he asked her sardonically.

'Good night,' she murmured – and turning her face from both of them, slipped back into an easy sleep.

The King of Hearts Casino wasn't the sort of place you'd take your old mother to – not unless she could afford to drop a couple of hundred pounds, anyway. The high-fliers didn't use it either: no one lost a fortune, or made one at the King of Hearts; it was strictly middle-of-the-road gambling. What it had in common with all other such clubs was the fact that the house always won: at the end of each noisy, smokey evening, the safe held a few thousand of the punters' pounds. It was a sure thing.

Harry and his workmate, Pete, stood across the street from their souped-up Jag and made a poor pretence of peering into a shop window – not that there were too many people about to observe the charade. They continued to admire last-year's fashions in a rundown boutique until a cleaner's van pulled up outside the casino, then waited until the driver had reached the front door. 'Here we go,' urged Harry, 'our cue.'

As they ran up to the casino, a third man, inside the Jag, fired the engine and made a U-turn, swerving in front of Glover's car as it came into the street. Harry and Pete pulled down ski-balaclavas to mask their faces, hammered the door, then smashed in as the bewildered cleaner opened it to them. 'Move back! Inside – quick!' The man dropped his brushes and pans as the gun in Harry's fist crossed his vision.

Going smoothly thought Glover. Then he saw two more cars power into the street. Harry and Pete, halfway through the casino door, saw them too: just as Doyle's car swung across the pavement to block the Jag.

Pete left the doorway at a dead run and Bodie dropped to one knee to steady his aim. 'Don't!' he yelled, then somersaulted back behind his car as a shot from Harry virtually breathed on him as it passed his ear. Doyle closed the trap from the far end of the street, sending his car back across the tarmac, hurling himself sideways as a shot from Pete shattered his windscreen, then clipping his man with answering fire.

Harry saw his chance. He lit off down the street, looking desperately for an escape route. Then he saw Glover's Cortina and pounded towards it, yelling, while Glover fought to turn between two parked cars. Harry's face loomed at the side window; he wrestled with the door, running alongside and shouting. Glover raised his gun and fired, watching the grimacing face drop away; then he slammed the accelerator to the floor and rocketed out of the street with Doyle – minus a windscreen – in pursuit.

Glover's advantage lay in the homework he'd done for the raid. He had driven the streets surrounding the casino a dozen times, noting the dead ends, the busy junctions. the bolt holes. He slammed through the gears, managing to find just enough speed to be out of sight of Doyle for thirty seconds – long enough to cut into a concealed laneway, stop the engine and watch Doyle pass him on the main street. He waited a minute, then reversed out. He was clear. Five more minutes and he'd found the camouflage of a traffic stream on the way back to his flat.

Under the same circumstances, many people would have headed in just the opposite direction; but Glover wasn't thinking clearly. He was scared – and his homing instinct was strong. Like a child pulling the blankets over his head, he wanted the security of his own place. Except it wasn't so secure.

Albie's Mercedes, with Ted at the wheel and Albie leaning casually on the bonnet, wasn't exactly an unobtrusive sight – but Glover, in a muck sweat of fright, failed to see it as he parked and made for his front door. Albie and Ted were across the road and on to him before he had a chance to register properly what was happening. He staggered under a blow, felt arms grab him from behind, then was whirled round. He looked past his attackers to see Doyle's car powering in at the entrance to the street and took his chance. 'The squad!' he bellowed.

Albie and Ted shot a glance towards Doyle, then tore back to the Merc, leaving Glover to dive through a hedge and make off across some gardens. Doyle braked heavily, trying to decide which to go for, then opted for the Merc and gunned off in pursuit. He reached the set of lights in time to see the big car picking up speed the other side of an impenetrable traffic jam. Horns honked and lights flashed as Doyle cut across the bows of irate drivers; then the thicket of vehicles closed round him.

Doyle swore. He swore lengthily, and inventively, and with real feeling.

This time, Glover thought things out more carefully. The first thing to do was contact Duffy. The girl at the club that Duffy had taken a shine to – she'd know.

It took him half an hour of keeping to the back-streets and doubling back now and then to make sure he wasn't being followed before he got to Morgan's apartment. He thumbed the bell anxiously.

'I'll get it!' Sylvie half-opened the door, then stepped back as Glover pushed in.

'Sorry I had to come round,' he gabbled. 'I got the address from the club. You know where he is – Duffy?'

'N-no,' she looked startled, '– how would I?'

Duffy didn't answer her directly. 'There's been a bit of a problem,' he went on. 'CI5 all over the flat. He quit.'

There was a tension between them that Morgan could plainly feel as he came into the room. He flushed with anger. 'What is it?' he demanded of Glover. 'What do you want?'

'Looking for Duffy.' Glover's attempt to sound tough wasn't too convincing. Morgan put a hand flat on the other man's chest and pushed. 'Yeah, well he's not here – right? And this is my flat.' The push became firmer: real muscle behind it. 'So if you don't mind ...' Glover felt the door against his back. 'Cool it,' he said with a quiver in his voice. 'It's all right ... all right ...' He fumbled with the door knob and Morgan gave him a last shove into the hallway, then slammed the door and turned on Sylvie.

'Are you insane?' His voice was rough. 'If Duffy's involved in an Organisation build-up, you're playing with fire!'

'What's that,' she countered, '– ancient loyalties talking?'

Morgan grabbed her and yanked her towards him

viciously. 'I'm on no one's side. I owe *them* nothing.' He pushed her away, but held her with his eyes. 'Remember that,' he said.

'John Albie. Fifty. Service in Berlin, the Congo. Mercenary recruit. Now runs a travel agency ...' Cowley's staccato briefing was interrupted as Doyle leaned forward to provide some secondary information '... which has suddenly closed up.'

'As everything else seems to have done,' added Bodie.

Cowley was holding a mug-shot of Albie, tapping the photograph against his thumb-nail. 'We've had tags on him before. He's been with the Organisation for a while.' Cowley was recalling the file information.

'Top cat,' said Bodie – he'd read the file too; he'd also tangled with the Organisation before. Albie was more than a list of statistics to him.

'You tried his family, friends?' Cowley wanted to know.

'Nothing!' said Doyle.

'What about the three boys who did the raid?'

'Third party,' Doyle told him. 'They do the hit and get a few quid for their pains. But they see no one.'

'And the Organisation gets its funds,' said Bodie bitterly.

Cowley tried to find a path through the jungle of false leads. 'What about the tip-off? Morgan?'

Doyle shrugged; it was a possibility. 'I don't know.'

Cowley decided to go for the one positive lead they *did* have. Morgan ... 'Get a stake-out on him,' he ordered. 'Find out who he eats, drinks and sleeps with. If he knows what's going on, that might lead us to it ... Twenty-four hours a day.' He stressed this last remark, then waved the photo of Albie: 'And find *him*!'

Given the urgency in Cowley's voice, it might have struck him as odd that Albie was in the process of deciding that he and Cowley should see each other face to face – as soon as possible. Seated uneasily in Ted's tastelessly furnished flat, and surrounded by posed pictures of second-rate heavyweight boxers, Albie was feeling a sense of discomfort that had nothing to do with Ted's insensitivity to interior decoration. He was beginning to feel the painful effect of Duffy's operations – beginning to feel pressured. And no one put the squeeze on Albie.

'Duffy's strangling us,' he said finally. 'They'll think it was us.' He watched gloomily as Ted gave over most of his attention to oiling a gleaming Smith & Wesson. 'Once they've got their teeth in, CI5 won't let go. We don't want a war ... and we can't lie low forever.'

'What'll we do?' asked Ted absently, checking the breech for grit.

'Fix another meet.' This got Ted's attention. 'And this time we will talk.' Albie paused. 'To Cowley.'

See and be seen – it was the golden rule for a meet like this. Bodie and Cowley walked on to the common at the appointed place and looked around at the treeless expanse of furze and grassy hillocks. 'Very reassuring,' remarked Bodie. 'The wide open spaces.'

They walked a little way to the top of a slight rise and turned to see Albie and Ted coming towards them. When there was no more than ten yards of cropped grass between the two parties, the new arrivals stopped.

'I'm not making promises after today,' Cowley's voice was firm.

'It's all been a mistake,' Albie smiled. 'The Organisation isn't operative. This is a good time for us. Things are ... politically favourable.'

'A gun robbery, an ambush and a funds hit,' countered Cowley.

Albie sighed mournfully. 'I know. I read the papers. Look ... take my word for it. Stop your boys nosing. Put a D-notice on the press. It's better for everyone if it's played down, otherwise everyone gets hysterical – my men, your men, the public.'

Bodie seemed amused by this plea for a quiet life. 'If it's not you.' he queried, 'who is it, then?'

'Our business,' asserted Albie. 'All I can say is you won't have any more trouble . . . take my word on that.'

Cowley turned away in disgust. Doing deals with villains – the idea choked him. Angry, he swung round to face Albie again. 'Let me tell you something!' The words came from between gritted teeth. 'One more smell of your lot and every Organisation man from here to Inverness spends Christmas in the nick.' He strode away, leaving Bodie to smile pleasantly at the fuming pair.

'Cheers,' he said brightly; then followed Cowley as he made for the road.

Ray Doyle was surprised to get the call – he'd judged that Morgan was too embittered ever to want to help the Squad; but you could never tell what hatred – or jealousy – could make a man do.

From the background noise on the R/T, Doyle guessed that the ex-CI5 man was phoning from the drinking club. '. . . no I'm not in a particularly generous mood,' Morgan was saying in answer to Doyle's tart question, 'it's just something I learned from a conversation with someone I hardly know. Can we meet? If you want the info it's yours.'

'All right,' Doyle couldn't afford to pass up the offer, but he remained suspicious. 'Why the change of heart?'

A pause; then – 'I just want to see someone who deserves to be pushed aside get what's coming . . . Right,' he concluded, 'see you then!' He hung up the phone and moved back into the club and made for the door. Behind him, unseen, Duffy put down his glass and followed.

CI5 were getting a lot of fresh air that day. Morgan had chosen a deserted spot on the edge of the countryside that borders north London. Trees, fields, birdsong, wildflowers . . . and the sound of Morgan's engine as he drove across the bumpy ground away from the main road and towards a disused quarry screened by bushes. He pulled up, got out of the car and looked back anxiously towards the road, just in time to catch a glimpse of a second car moving off the road above his position and sliding behind a small spinney. He began to walk uphill towards the trees, conscious of the fact that he was wide-open to attack. As he came closer, he called out: 'Doyle?' He took a couple more steps, then froze. Duffy's car.

He started to run – sheer self-preservation made his legs work, sent him stumbling over the tufty grass towards cover – but he knew it was hopeless. Before he was half-way back, a shot rang out. Morgan felt the bullet as a vast blow in the back; there was a moment's pain, then things fell away as they do under anaesthesia: a lurch, blackness, a fraction of a second of noise and colour and then Morgan toppled sideways as his legs lost their strength. He was dead before his face smashed into the grass.

Duffy kept the rifle levelled – supported in a 'V' of branches – until he saw his victim drop. Then his head snapped round as he heard the second car. Doyle could see Morgan's body before he was even out of the driving seat. He came out of the car low, gun drawn, his searching look travelling from one piece of cover to the next.

Duffy, unseen, watched in amazement; then his look changed to one of unalloyed delight. Nestling the rifle barrel back into its support, he sighted carefully ...

At first, Bodie saw nothing but the two cars parked down the slope from a dense spinney. He parked and got out. Then Doyle's head appeared, half-hidden by couch grass that fringed the hollow where he was hiding.

Bodie grinned. 'What's up with you? Get caught short?'

Wordlessly, Doyle jerked his head back and Bodie followed the gesture to where Morgan's body lay, half-concealed by a dip in the ground. Then he straightened up and faced his partner. Back in the spinney, Duffy saw his chance of a clear shot at Doyle ruined as Bodie's body came across his line of fire. He hesitated: two quick, accurate shots? Or one shot followed by a game of cat and mouse! Silently, he eased the gun back and made for his car.

George Cowley was a deeply worried man. Murder ... now murder had to be added to the list of crimes in this case. If someone was playing a game, he reflected sourly, then the rules were being invented to suit the action. Bodie's conviction that the Organisation was active again and fitting-out their men – maybe; Doyle's notion of a runner, someone with a grudge – perhaps. Or a lone wolf, that was always possible. Whatever the truth, though, things were being made hot for Cowley; and that he didn't like.

Forsaking his thoughts, he gave his attention to the photographs Bodie was flicking through.

'From the stake-out on Morgan,' said the agent, handing the first shot to his chief. 'Negative ... negative ...' he handed them over one by one: '... that's a lady collecting for the new town hall ... That's –' Bodie frowned and took back the photo. 'She's familiar.'

Doyle looked over his shoulder and made the identification: 'His lady-friend. Sylvie.'

Bodie remembered: 'Works at the drinking club.'

'I checked her,' Doyle interjected. 'Looks okay. No nasty connections on file.'

Bodie continued to sift through the prints: Morgan talking in a shop doorway; Morgan filling his car at a garage; Morgan buying a newspaper; Morgan outside a pub doorway with Duffy ... Bodie passed over it, but Doyle retrieved it, and looked at it thoughtfully while Cowley took issue with Bodie. 'Yesterday I told you to put a twenty-four-hour watch on Morgan. Why didn't you?'

'We did,' retorted Bodie, 'but he gave us the slip, like the old pro he is.'

'Was,' put in Doyle idly; he was sorting offhandedly through the pile of pictures that Bodie had labelled 'negative'.

'Maybe Morgan was Albie's vendetta,' suggested Bodie. 'Maybe that's why he stopped a bullet.'

'I know this face.' Doyle was still scrutinising the photo of Morgan and Duffy.

'If you do, Criminal Records don't,' said Bodie.

'... but from where?' Doyle continued. Then he reached over and picked up the photo of Sylvie ... Sylvie, taken at the club!

She looked a lot different from the smiling girl in the telephoto lens shot: dishevelled, scared, her hair awry, she sat right on the edge of the hard wooden chair as Ted hovered threateningly over her. Albie perched casually on the edge of the table: casually, but too close for comfort.

'... I hardly knew him.' She'd been trying to convince them for some time. 'There's nothing else I can tell you.'

Albie looked at Ted, who shrugged. The girl was probably telling the truth; it wouldn't do any harm, he though, to rough her up a bit – just to make quite sure.

'Please.' Her hands were trembling. 'I want to go. I don't know where Duffy is!'

Albie looked at her with deceptive gentleness. 'You're a big girl now. You work at "Sparklers" and you know who dabbles in what. You know how the Organisation works.' She didn't respond, so he went on: 'Duffy was in the Organisation up north – in another group. Then there was a split. He didn't see eye to eye with our political policies and he wanted a war that we didn't.' Albie paused for effect before saying: 'He still wants it! And the longer he remains – doing what *he* wants to do – the more chance he has of creating a dangerous situation.' His tone softened now; he seemed almost to be pleading. 'No one wants that kind of war, Sylvie. Help us stop Duffy.'

Abruptly, he moved away from her: she was being dismissed and was quick to seize the opportunity. Ted passed her handbag to her with exaggerated politeness as she sidled slowly towards the door.

By the time she hit the street, she was half-running: her speed almost taking Doyle by surprise. He let the clutch in snappily and coasted his car away from the side-street where he'd been waiting, following the frightened girl until she reached a bus-stop and stood there looking agitated. He steered into the kerb and rolled the window down.

'Care to get in?' Startled, she drew away; then looked hostile when she realised it was Doyle. 'You must make a lot of friends at the club –' Doyle persisted. 'That was Albie's friend's pad you came out of. Mr Albie a friend of yours?' No response; instead, she made a point of busily looking up and down the road for her bus. Doyle wasn't about to give up: 'That how Morgan got his info – through you, from Albie?' He got out of the car and stood beside her, refusing to be ignored.

Suddenly, she flared up. 'None of this is any of my business. I just want to be left alone.'

Doyle responded by handing her the photograph of Morgan and Duffy. 'You know that man?' Silence. 'Tell me then: are you best chums with Albie, too – was that it?'

'I don't know him.' Her voice had ice in it. 'Either of them. My relationships are my own business. If you want to know about Morgan – go and ask him.'

Go and ask him . . . 'She doesn't know,' thought Doyle. 'My God, she doesn't know!'

Her bus arrived and she stepped aboard. All Doyle could think of to say was: 'You haven't seen Morgan . . . ?' Then the bus had gone and Sylvie with it.

Chapter Ten

There were ghosts in the deserted tenement building: the ghosts of people who had lived and died there, people who had fought and loved and suffered and been happy in those poky rooms and mean passageways. There were the ghosts of arrivals, of new starts, of failure; ghosts of words spoken in passion and of children's laughter. Ghosts – and now Glover invading their territory as he moved through the rubble-strewn corridors and into a small flat cluttered with broken furniture and the tatters of old newspapers.

There was utter silence; then the slightest of noises. Glover heard it and checked. There came an explosion of noise as Duffy leapt out at him from behind the broken door of an old wardrobe, his rifle trained from the hip. Glover stumbled back, near to screaming. When he found his voice, he asked: 'Are you *mad*?'

Duffy lowered the gun; then he laughed and let his body relax. 'Can't be too safe, now. Didn't know who you were.' He crossed to a grimy window. 'Sure you weren't followed?'

'I'm well practised, aren't I?' Glover was unwrapping a parcel, too angry from the fright to fall in with Duffy's suddenly genial mood. When the items were displayed on the floor, Duffy walked back to check them: two sausage shapes in heavy, greased paper; a coil of wire; a clock; detonators . . .

'We've done it, mate,' he said to Glover. 'On our tod. We've started the war. After this, nothing'll stop it. CI5 will want their blood sacrifice and every Organisation man will be armed and active.'

As he was speaking, he rapidly combined the ingredients of the bomb – working quickly and with a skill that came from familiarity. When he'd finished he hefted the deadly bundle, tossing it gently from hand to hand and giggling when Glover put out a nervous, restraining hand. 'We won,' he said through his laughter; then his voice became suddenly cold: 'And Doyle's out there. At the front. Every time the Organisation moves, he moves. Which is what we want, eh?' There was real, maniacal passion in his next words: 'More than anything – Ray Doyle.'

Glover's thoughts were elsewhere. 'They'll come gunning for us after this,' he said. 'Our own lot.'

Duffy placed a friendly hand on his shoulder. 'They'll be too busy ducking a crossfire.' He stopped, as if lost for words, then said: 'You've been a good mate, Glover. When the Organisation wouldn't fight my fight, you did.'

'We have different aims, you know that. I believe the boys should be operative.'

It sounded like a rejection and a shadow of anger passed over Duffy's face. Then he laughed once more, and his mood became animated. He crossed the room and fetched a large-scale map of the city. 'The ideal spot for that bomb –' he jabbed a finger, 'the new Government offices in Darrow Lane.' Glover took the map from him, studying it, looking uneasy while Duffy continued: 'Six o'clock it goes off. I ring the Squad at five-to. And Doyle gets his. You plant it ... and bring Sylvie to me.' He frowned. 'I don't trust her ... after Morgan.'

'But she'll only be deadweight ...' Glover began.

Duffy's mood changed again: 'Don't argue,' he shouted, 'bring her!' He fought with himself to make it a request. 'Please,' he said softly, 'like a mate.' And he handed Glover the bomb.

'Ballistics say Morgan was shot with a bullet from the unrecovered gun.' Doyle raised an eyebrow at Cowley, wondering what his chief would make of the information.

'You wanted to help Morgan,' Cowley reasoned, 'and he decided to give some. He was going to blow the whistle on someone and that someone killed him. Logically, it was the same someone who hit that gun shop ...'

Doyle completed the train of thought: 'And the Organisation claim it has nothing to do with them.'

'And who do we believe?' Cowley worried at the problem. 'Maybe those boys are laughing up their sleeves at us. Maybe this *is* the start of a build-up.'

He looked enquiringly at Bodie, who took his cue. 'You know my feelings – start hitting back. Now. Before it gets into full swing.'

Cowley's look switched to Doyle: asking the same question. 'Give it twenty-four hours,' came the response. 'Keep up the stake-outs on Organisation people. Wait!'

Bodie opened his mouth to oppose this, but Cowley waved him to silence. 'Once we start moving it's a war,' he reminded the agent. 'This city can't afford that war.'

'Duffy wants to see you.' Glover had found Sylvie at the club, catching her between customers to pass on Duffy's message. She was flustered: unsure, now, about exactly what was going on. 'I've been looking for him,' she replied. 'I phoned his flat again and again.'

'He had to ...' Glover hesitated, 'to leave. Can you come now? He wants you.'

She seemed unsure; then said, 'All right. Where is he?'

'Come on,' Glover took her elbow and began to steer her to the door. 'I'll take you.'

The drive had bewildered her – into a part of the city that was strange to her; but her apprehension grew minute by minute as Glover led her through rank alleyways to the door of the ratty apartment. He tapped at the door and ushered her in among the junk and decaying furniture. Duffy came forward, put his arm round her and pecked her on the cheek.

'Did you set it?' This first to Glover, who nodded. 'Great!' Then he turned his attention to the girl:

'Apologies for the regal splendour,' he quipped, 'the butler's on holiday.' He led them both over to a table bearing a bottle of Scotch and some glasses. 'C'mon – have a drink.'

Sylvie found her voice: 'I tried to call you. You know – obviously – that everyone's looking for you. Albie talked to me ... someone had seen me at the club with you.' Duffy's face tightened. '... and CI5,' she told him.

He stopped in the middle of pouring a drink. 'What about CI5?' He smiled stiffly. '*They* didn't pull you in?'

'A man called Doyle was tailing me. He used to work with Morgan when ...'

Duffy exploded – and this time there was an edge of hysteria in his voice. 'Doyle! You said Doyle?' She nodded. 'You didn't tell me Morgan was ex-CI5! You said ex-police! You mean, they knew each other – well?' Again she nodded, afraid to break in on his tirade. 'They pulled you in?' He swung round and snapped 'Check!' at Glover – indicating the window. 'Check, for God's sake!'

'We weren't followed,' Glover told him; even so, he went over to the window and looked out. Duffy grabbed Sylvie. 'What did you say? What did you tell Doyle? He knows me? Come on!' He shook her roughly.

'You're hurting me!' Suddenly, she was frightened. 'I said nothing! He had a photograph ...'

Duffy released her – abandoned her, turning away, thinking hard. 'He knows ... Doyle knows ... He has me ...' Again, he turned to Sylvie. 'You told him nothing?'

'What *could* I have told him?' She was humouring him now; as one humours a lunatic.

'Forty minutes ...' Duffy looked at his watch, then to Glover. 'Forty minutes!' He walked across the room and picked up a battered leather holdall. Sitting down on one of the ruined sofas, he drew out a dog-eared scrapbook into which were pasted a number of newspaper cuttings. There was an unspeakable tension in him as he looked at them. Sylvie was drawn by curiosity – by his manner. He thrust the book at her. 'That was Doyle,' he snarled, 'he did that.' One of the more prominent headlines ran: ORGANISATION BOY KILLED BY SQUAD MAN. Duffy smoothed the creases in the yellowed clippings with a strange, loving care. 'Five years ago,' he said, his voice a savage whisper. 'A bank haul. My brother got a bullet in the brain.' His eyes took on a look of undiluted hatred. He turned to Glover. 'You get him here!'

'No.' Glover spoke the word quietly and Duffy seemed not to hear him. His words seemed to come from very far away. 'You know ... it took me all this time to find out who pulled the trigger. And then a friend – a poor old sod like Morgan who was once on the inside – he told me. Ray Doyle.' He made the name sound like a curse. 'And you know what the Organisation said when I told them Ray Doyle did it? They said "Too bad". And I said "Blow the man apart."' He turned to Duffy once more. 'Get him here. Glover – you take her out. Ring him; code it. No! Let her ring. Tell him ... tell him you know Morgan's informant. Tell him you want a meet.'

'That's crazy,' said Glover. 'The bomb's enough ...'

'He's not looking for the bomb, is he?' screamed Duffy. 'He's looking for me! Supposing he doesn't go there ...' He became calm again – falsely calm. 'No. You get him here.'

Glover watched Duffy's hand flexing around the stock of the rifle that lay beside him. He knew the man had gone over the top; there was no reasoning with him now – no holding him. He got up and took Sylvie's arm to lead her out of the room. As the door closed, Duffy transferred his grip from the gun to the whisky bottle.

'A call for you 4.5' – Doyle's R/T crackled into life. 'Public telephone ... a woman ... won't give her name.'

Doyle pressed the switch on the transceiver. 'Switch her through.'

'Mr Doyle?' He recognised Sylvie's voice.

'That's right.'

'I thought I should phone you ... you being a friend of Morgan's and ... after you talked to me – well, you wanted to know who Morgan's been talking to.'

'And you want to talk to me?'

'Can we meet?'

'Sure,' replied Doyle easily. 'Where?'

No one's lived here for a decade or more thought Doyle as he approached the tenements. He revised the thought – tramps, maybe, winos ... But why would she want to meet here? He climbed the stairs to the room Duffy had comandeered, moving warily through corridors, skirting piles of trash as he approached Duffy's door.

'Sylvie?' His voice echoed in the empty building. She appeared at once, coming through the door, then standing there, pale but apparently calm. Then she took a couple of steps towards him.

'What's this?' asked Doyle, 'squatters' haven?'

She improvised: 'Yes ... I've friends who stay here.'

Doyle noticed the tension behind her attempt to be conversational. 'Look,' he said, 'I want you to know something. If you're scared about grassing on anyone, don't be. What happened to Morgan was a million-to-one chance. He knew ...'

He got no further. 'What do you mean?' Her eyes widened. 'What ... *what* happened to him?'

Doyle watched her face, looking for the bluff. He found nothing. 'You know he's dead? Shot.'

A long moment passed while she took the information in. 'Who ...' she began. Then – 'Run! Now! Run – get out!'

Doyle's turn to be shocked. He hesitated long enough for Duffy to spring into view, the rifle at his hip. Doyle's reactions were restored to him. He leaped forward and pulled Sylvie down as three ear-splitting shots crashed over their heads. 'You murdering bastard!' shrieked Duffy.

Doyle's gun gave answering fire, sending Duffy scurrying back into the flat, passing Glover who had drawn his hand gun. As Duffy made for the fire-escape to the roof, Glover leaned out of the doorway to get a shot at Doyle. A bullet from Doyle's Browning took him full in the chest, dropping him instantly. Leaving Sylvie cowering on the floor of the passageway, Doyle scrambled to his feet and took off after Duffy.

He got within sight of the flat roof with its tall chimney-stacks and knew Duffy would be under cover, waiting. A couple of shots proved him right – taking out chunks of brickwork near his head when he dived for cover himself. He flattened himself behind one of the chimneys and waited for the other man to make a move. Nothing.

'Duffy!' he tried, 'C'mon – we're a mile ahead of you. What did you think? – That you'd get an Organisation war going on a grudge fight?' Another slug from the rifle scarred the bricks. 'C'mon,' Doyle urged. 'The game's up. We've been through these runs before – your boys and ours. Waste of time for you ...'

He waited. Still nothing. Things had been quiet for too long and he decided to risk a look. He saw nothing but a vista of chimneys and rubble and ventilator shafts – no Duffy, no gunfire either. Inch by inch he crawled forward, praying that the man hadn't worked his way back for a clear shot.

In fact, that's just what Duffy had done – circling to come up behind Doyle; and now he had the CI5 man squarely in his sights. '*Now* – Doyle!' – a yell of triumph as his fingers tightened on the trigger, his foot braced against the very edge of the roof. All things except equal, Doyle was a dead man there and then; except that no one – least of all Duffy – had considered Sylvie.

Her push hit him in the chest: both hands slamming

into his breastbone. For a few horrific seconds he teetered on the parapet, seeming to hang in the air; then the gun went off, its recoil enough to finish the job. He fell soundlessly out into space, his eyes wide with shock and terror.

The bullet had smashed into Sylvie's arm; her scream was still in Doyle's ears as he rushed to the edge and looked over. Duffy's body lay spreadeagled on the pavement some sixty feet below. 'Yeah – Duffy old pal.' Doyle's voice held no emotion at all.

'The bomb ...' He whirled round as Sylvie's anguished voice cut in on his thoughts. 'They set a bomb – him and Glover – for six o'clock.'

Trying not to show his tension, Doyle propped her against one of the chimney stacks and examined the wound. 'It's all right. You're okay.' He could see that the slug had broken no bones. 'Tell me about the bomb. Where is it? Did he say?'

'Government offices,' she said through her pain, 'Darrow Lane ... the car park.'

'All right. You rest here. I'll get help.' He checked his watch and set off towards the fire-escape at a run.

Doyle reached his car in less than a minute and checked the electric dashboard clock while he rapped out a message on the R/T. It was 5.56!

'4.5. to 3.7 ... 4.5 to 3.7. Over.' There was a jumble of static. He yelled, angrily: 'Bodie!'

'All right, I read –' Bodie's voice. 'Keep your shirt on.'

'Get an "all out" – bomb squad, the lot,' Doyle bellowed. 'General warning. Bomb in Darrow Lane, set for six.'

The banter went out of Bodie's voice immediately. 'Darrow Lane. On my way. General call ...' Doyle didn't wait to hear the rest. His racing start took him down the alleyway with a shrill scream of scorching tyres. He glanced down again at the clock: 5.57. Recklessly he cut through the light traffic, mounting the pavement and leaving other drivers cursing as he covered the two blocks to the elegant Darrow Lane offices. He screamed past the police cordon that had already been set up, slewed into the car park and left the driver's seat before the car had properly come to a halt. Bodie was a second or two before him, yelling at the uniformed men to control the inevitable crowd that had started to collect.

'Get 'em back,' he yelled. 'There's a bomb under here somewhere. Back!' Then he began to trot along the lines of parked cars, looking for anything that might be the bomb: any parcel, bundle, an old coat – anything concealing. Doyle ran up to join him. 'Any luck? Anything at all ... ?' he gasped.

Bodie merely said: 'I hope your grass had his locations right.' They split up, to cover the ground more effectively, trying to combine speed with efficiency. Precious seconds ticked by. Then Bodie saw it – not a package, not disguised as anything, just a naked bomb, clock attached and plainly in view. It showed 5.59!

'Here!' he called hoarsely. Doyle sprinted over and caught sight of the clock. 'Six! It'll go at six,' his tone was hushed.

'What is it?' asked Bodie. 'Standard – gelignite ...' He reached down and lifted the bomb with infinite care. 'Clock,' he noted, 'no dummy wire ...'

'Leave it,' Doyle suggested; but there was no time to run now; the second hand was ticking away the last minute.

Another car sped into the parking lot – Cowley! Doyle turned long enough to yell, 'Get out!' Then looked back at Bodie, who was still attempting to size up the bomb. 'Detonator ...' he muttered, fingering the connection. Doyle leaned forward and grasped the wires. 'Try it ... pull them,' he snapped; then, when Bodie hesitated, yanked them himself.

In a booby-trapped bomb, pulling the detonators is as fatal as waiting for them to do their work in the usual way; with gelignite, in any case, nothing is certain;

Doyle knew that it was a pretty efficient method of committing suicide – or at least making it a safe odds-on bet. One factor prompted him as he pulled the wires ... the second-hand on the clock showed one clear division before the twelve: and there isn't so much at stake when you're betting at odds-on if you've nothing to lose.

The wires came free; the clock moved to six; there was a dull *clack-clack*; the world stayed in one piece. Ridiculously, Doyle was conscious of the *chirrup* of a London sparrow scavenging for food on the concrete paving of the car park. Both men looked at the bomb for a long time, the tension slowly draining from them. Then Bodie said: 'Bang.'

'Yeah,' Doyle replied, then – as Cowley reached them – eased back the plastic detonator sleeve. It was empty! He held it out for the others to see. 'No detonator,' he said needlessly. No one laughed.

'I heard the call,' said Cowley finally. 'Duffy?'

'Yeah.' Doyle was still turning the bomb over in his hands, wonderingly. 'Double-ended vendetta,' he said, 'get me and get back at the Organisation who wouldn't take up his fight.'

'Clever boy,' Cowley observed, 'he could have brought this city down round our ears.

Bodie pursed his lips. 'Not clever enough to remember the detonator on a simple 1-2-3 bomb though, was he?'

'Situation defused.' Doyle underlined the point by letting the useless wires dangle from his fingers.

Bodie looked thoughtful. 'For the time being, anyway,' he remarked. There was a fighting look in his eyes. This time the Organisation was in the clear; but there would be other times – Bodie knew it. Other times – and other wars to fight.

Chapter Eleven

The dip had been working with routine efficiency for twenty minutes or so and knew that the time had come to quit. Twenty minutes, half-an-hour – it was quite long enough in one area. Some marks might go half a day without realising they'd had their pockets picked, but there was always the risk that someone would reach for a wallet to check a rail ticket or a theatre booking. No more than five minutes on any pitch, no more than half an hour in one part of a town: that way you could pick up a couple of hundred and stay out of trouble.

Windsor was prime territory in the tourist season. Crowded streets packed with visitors who were enjoying themselves too much to be properly wary: and the Americans, in particular, were given to carrying their wallets and bill-folds in a hip pocket. Easy stuff. Then, of course, there was the castle; the pickings there were choice, with everyone rubbernecking at the bearskins, scarlet tunics and the crashing boots that threatened to shatter the cobbles. He'd been working the crowd watching the sentry-change for a few minutes, pausing now and then to give the impression of enjoying the spectacle himself, before relieving the honest citizens of their money. He was in the process of taking a wallet from the jackpot pocket of a German tourist, when the man chose to reach into that pocket himself – gripping not the expected flash-bulb, but the pickpocket's hand! He hung on, wheeling round to confront the thief, and a weird tug of war ensued for a moment; then the dip managed to pull free, crashing through the crowd with the irate German in full cry.

'*Polizei!* Poleeze!' The pickpocket – fitter and younger – had reached the fringe of the crowd and was heading towards a covered way that would take him into a more crowded part of the town. Nearby, a policeman, who was giving directions to another tourist, heard the yelling and looked up. He knew immediately what had happened ... lost children, people wandering into the forbidden parts of the castle grounds and the occasional pickpocket were the stock-in-trade of the middle-aged coppers assigned to castle duties. He gave chase as best he could, puffing as his waddling run took him to the entrance of the covered way.

The thief was almost at the other end and going like the wind. He cast a glance over his shoulder to make sure that no one was likely to catch him and, as he did so, collided with a pretty, dark-haired girl who had walked in from the far entrance, sending her flying together with guide-books, street-map and an expensive-looking 8mm cine-camera. She sprawled there a minute, stunned, then collected her belongings as if nothing had happened and began to walk away, as the policeman arrived black in the face and ready to give up the chase. He took out his R/T to report the crime; then noticed that the girl's map still lay on the floor. By this time she was twenty or thirty yards away. He picked up the map and called after her, but she made no response. 'Doesn't speak English,' he thought. 'Well, I'm not running after her too.' He yelled again: 'Oi!' and waved the map in the air.

A passer-by, seeing this charade going on, grabbed the girl's arm, trying to point out what was happening. She shook the man off and quickened her pace. 'Oh, Lord,' thought the copper hopelessly, 'she thinks she's done something wrong.' He trotted after her as best he could. 'Your map, dear,' he bellowed, still waving it in the air.

The girl quickened her pace: going at a run now. A second passer-by also tried to stop her and she knocked him away; but, in doing so, she stumbled and fell, giving the policeman enough time to come within a few feet of her. Fumbling in her handbag, she produced a small automatic pistol. As the policeman reached her, she turned and without any hesitation fired at point-blank range.

The look of disbelief on the policeman's face changed rapidly to one of shock and pain; then there was no sort of expression at all. He was dead before his body came to rest on the paving-stones. The girl stood there a second, the gun still held at arm's length, then she turned, intending to run.

Before she could get into her stride, a man stepped out of the crowd with a drawn gun in his hand. 'Stop or I'll fire!' Whether or not she understood what he said, the tone was unmistakable. Without even bothering to look at him, the girl started to attempt the impossible. She'd gone no more than ten yards when his bullet took her in the back, kicking her a further two or three yards along the pavement before she pitched on to her face, skidded a short way and lay still. The man with the gun ran up to her, waving back the small knot of sightseers who had begun to circle the body. 'Police. Keep back,' he said briefly. Then he bent over the girl. She was dead; he'd known she would be dead. It wasn't the shot he'd been going for – but she had been swerving as she ran. Sighing, he picked up the automatic she'd dropped, using a handkerchief to keep his fingerprints off the weapon. Then he collected the rest of her belongings – including the cine-camera that lay near her outstretched hand.

Chapter Twelve

The briefing room was cool and quiet and dim. Very little light managed to penetrate the heavy curtains and almost nothing could be heard of the busy traffic in Whitehall. A small screen had been set up at one end of the long table and the whir of a projector heralded a flickering view of an exclusive Mayfair mews.

Cowley's voice competed with the clattering machine. 'Yesterday, at Windsor, a girl shot a policeman. She herself was killed by a detective coming off duty from routine "Royals protection". This film was in the girl's possession.'

He stopped to allow the film to tell its own story. The footage was amateurish, badly focused, but workmanlike. It began with a too-long shot of the mews, then moved shakily upwards to reveal a TV aerial mechanic on a nearby roof. The man wasn't adjusting wires, though, or fixing brackets; he was assembling a sniper's rifle!

Next, the amateur camera-man showed a builder's van parked half-way along the mews; a face appeared briefly at the rear window. Then there were more jerky camera movements which revealed watchers in the windows of neighbouring houses.

Another change in direction brought two cars into focus, driving through the arch at the end of the mews. As they passed the builder's van, it swung across the street, effectively blocking them and stopping anything else pulling into the mews. Immediately, a minicab, closer to the camera, pulled across the mews at the near end, providing a total screen. The two cars pulled up outside one of the mews houses and disgorged six tall, powerfully built men who clustered round a tall figure in trench coat and dark glasses who had climbed out of the first car. Surrounding their charge from all sides, like participants in a rugby scrum, they hustled him into the house. There remained a few pointless moments of wasted footage, then the film petered out. Cowley stepped into the glare of the projector light.

'As you have probably gathered,' he said, 'that was a security operation.' Bodie and Doyle, seated further down the table, offered no comment. Cowley continued: 'Fortunately, it was only a rehearsal. But the fact that it was illicitly filmed is a matter of grave concern to HMG.' He snapped his fingers and a slide appeared on the screen behind him, part of it taking the contours of his shoulder and head. He stepped to one side and the picture slid crisply into focus. It showed two men: one tall and thin, dressed in casual clothes apart from the Palestinian head-cloth that framed his narrow face; the other sporting combat gear.

'On the left,' Cowley indicated the taller man, 'Kemel Khadi, now recognised as the leader of moderate Palestinian opinion. A man who enjoys the favour of both the Saudis and the oil emirates.' His tone took on a measure of urgency. 'Khadi's due here on Thursday at the special invitation of the FO, for secret talks which could vitally affect British interests in the Middle East.'

'And somebody's blown the whistle?' deduced Doyle.

'On a grand scale, if that film's anything to go by,' Cowley agreed.

Bodie chipped in now: 'And that was where the meet was going to take place?' He waved a hand towards the screen that had borne the fuzzy pictures of the activity in the mews.

'Yes,' Cowley confirmed. 'Now there's an odds-on chance it won't take place at all. Khadi's taking a great risk coming here.' Turning back to the screen, he pointed at the man in fatigues. 'No one knows that better than the heavy on the right. Aziz Doad. He's Khadi's Head of Security.' *And obviously no pussy-cat,* thought Doyle, taking in the muscular build, the hard eyes, the air of readiness that was apparent even in the photograph.

'Almost certainly, that film was taken for a Palestinian group opposed to Khadi's fraternisation with the West,' Cowley continued. 'There's every reason to believe an attempt will be made on Khadi's life while he is in London. If Doad gets wind of it, he'll tell his boss not to come.'

'And he won't,' stated Doyle, his eyes still fixed on Doad's photo.

'Correct,' said Cowley.

'So – find the leak?' Bodie was anxious to get things moving.

'Right!' Cowley became businesslike. 'Outside the UK the arrangements are known only to Khadi's immediate staff. At this end, apart from the Foreign Office, the only person who knew of Khadi's plans was Colonel Roger Masterson, MP – well-known for his pro-Arab stance.' The slide of Khadi and Doad was replaced with another of Masterson, wearing the same kind of head-dress as Khadi had affected. The MP was standing next to Khadi in a posed snapshot. 'Masterson was instrumental in setting up the visit,' Cowley told them. 'He is a personal friend of Khadi's.'

The next slide was not a snapshot, and it was very far from being posed. The dead girl lay in an ugly, crumpled heap on the paving stones, her limbs twisted in the ungainliness of violent death. 'Our other lead,' announced Cowley. 'The girl arrived at Heathrow last Monday. Came from Madrid. Her passport states that she's Pilar Hernandez, a student. It's a forgery. Neither Interpol nor the European terrorist indices have any trace ...' A new slide showed a slightly dowdy terrace in Notting Hill. 'She spent one night at the YWCA and then rented a room in this building.' A further slide – this time of a strikingly pretty girl in airline stewardess's uniform. '... In a flat owned by one Shelley Hunter, an American working for an executive air service based in London. She hasn't shown up on any of the indices either.'

'So all we have to do,' commented Doyle wryly, 'is wrap

up a major terrorist conspiracy in forty-eight hours with virtually nothing to go on?'

'That's the bad news,' Cowley agreed. 'The good news is: the girl's down to you.' Doyle brightened a little. In fact, he brightened rather a lot. Bodie neither smiled nor spoke – which was probably just as well.

He was still unsmiling when he knocked at Shelley Hunter's door an hour later. She was down to Doyle ... that meant that he had to play the official role; and when he saw that Shelley was even prettier in life than in her photograph, he knew it wasn't at all the role he wanted to play. He showed her his ID and she let him into the flat with a show of reluctance. 'Thanks,' she said acidly, nodding towards a forensic man who was trotting to and fro with mysterious little boxes, '... thanks, but I already have one.'

'Looks as if there's room for two,' Bodie retorted, looking round the spacious apartment. 'Anyway, English policemen ...'

'... are wonderful.' She finished the cliché for him, adding: 'I used to think so, too.' As they went into the sitting-room, she elaborated her annoyance. 'Boy, what a put-on. I let a room to a little "nebbish" who looks like a nun off limits. Then I get back from a one night stop-over in Brussels and what do I find? *Sister* Pilar's been blowing cops away.' She took a bottle of duty-free Scotch out of an airline bag and held it up to Bodie in a silent question. He shook his head. 'How did you meet her?' he asked.

Shelley changed the Scotch for a box of 'air-side' Lucky Strike and broke it open. 'I put this ad in the evening paper. You know – the usual flat sharing kind of deal.' Bodie shook his head to the Luckies, too. 'And she just walked in off the street?'

'Right. Like I said: she seemed a nice kid.'

'She tell you anything about herself?'

'Music student, I think.' Bodie looked doubtful.

'Look,' Shelley told him, 'I'm out of town a lot. I liked the idea of someone being around the place. We have a lot of burglaries in this district you know.'

'She pay cash?'

'On the button!'

Bodie turned it all over in his mind for a short while; then he said simply: 'Okay' and headed for the door. He turned when he reached it, and was treated to the sight of Shelley bending over to retrieve something from the airline bag, one knee lifted and resting on a chair, her hip canted over to lend a provocative swerve to an already very sexy outline. On the seat of her delectably tight jeans were sewn three flower patches. Bodie enjoyed the view for a long minute. *That's the only sort of pansy that'll rest there,* he thought, eyeing the patches on the stretched denim. Then he said, 'Miss Hunter, could you make sure that he takes everything belonging to the late "Sister" Pilar?' – nodding towards the man from forensics.

'Sure!' Shelley held the pose as she answered. Bodie's turn to brighten.

Roger Masterson lived, as MPs tend to, in a 'better' part of town. His house was decently large, without being showy, and its tasteful furnishings included a few Arabic objets d'art. As he ushered Cowley towards a door at the end of a long corridor hung with unobtrusive canvases, he was saying: 'Frances Cottingham has been my secretary for over ten years. I trust her totally.'

'Are you sure she's the only person who's been told, Colonel Masterson?'

'Look Cowley, Khadi is a personal friend of mine and I am only too aware of the risk he's taking in coming here,' replied the MP tartly. 'Moreover, as I set up the visit it's I who will be blamed if anything goes wrong.'

Cowley's tone was dry: 'Not exclusively, Colonel, I assure you ...'

Masterson gave him a look, then knocked on the door

and threw it open. Frances Cottingham looked startled at the sight of a second man with her employer. Then the handsome features composed themselves and she offered a half-quizzical smile of greeting. She was rarely less than composed: and 'handsome' was just the right adjective for her strong, pleasant face. She was dressed, as always, in quiet good taste; but there was a sadness behind her composure – sadness and a measure of tension that could always be detected. Frances Cottingham had the look of a woman whom life is beginning to pass by – and who knows it.

'Frances, Mr Cowley – CI5,' said Masterson, making the introductions. 'He'd like a word; would you mind?'

She pushed aside the pad she'd been doodling on when they entered and her look grew more confused. 'I ... er ... No, I suppose not ...' Masterson left them together.

'Just routine,' Cowley smiled at himself, inwardly, for using the old 'Just routine' routine. The odd thing was, so many people were reassured by it. 'May I ...?' He indicated a chair on the other side of her desk, then took it when she nodded. 'You will appreciate, Miss Cottingham, that the circumstances of Mr Khadi's forthcoming visit are unusual ...' By this time, she was fully in control, watching him carefully, her arms placidly folded. He continued: '... Normally this kind of meeting is the sole concern of the Foreign Office. In such a situation, the security arrangements are straightforward.'

'What are you implying, Mr Cowley?' she asked coldly.

'I'm implying that I have to be sure there's no accidental leak of information.'

'Are you suggesting I gossip?' She asked the question as if the notion amused her.

'No,' Cowley insisted. 'A letter left near a window,' he tapped the pad she'd been doodling on, 'the odd, revealing doodle tossed into the wastepaper basket. That's all it takes.'

She was dismissive. 'The Colonel and I have a simple

rule in situations like these. We keep no documentary records of any kind.'

Cowley matched her tone for coolness. 'A highly disciplined procedure,' he said, managing to leave the impression that he doubted it.

'Foolproof, Mr Cowley,' replied Frances Cottingham. A slight stress on the first syllable permitted the insult without running the risk of a rebuke. *Nicely done,* thought Cowley and mentally doffed his hat.

Ray Doyle was experiencing an altogether less subtle encounter. He'd lugged his battered suitcase upstairs to the door of the flat he'd rented: in the same house as Shelley Hunter and just one floor below. As he fumbled for the key, a door opened across the landing and a woman emerged, wearing battered slippers, a stained apron and a battered, stained face to match. She regarded the agent for a while, then croaked: 'You new?'

'Yup.' Doyle searched another pocket as she limped forward, switching from one arm to the other the black cat she was cradling. *A couple of centuries ago,* thought Doyle, *she'd have run a great risk of being burnt at the stake.* She peered at him, then: 'You're on the telly, ain't you?'

'Not me, love,' Doyle tried a winning smile, 'I'm a student.'

'Funny ...' she wasn't to be put off. 'I'd swear I've seen you on Coronation Street.'

There was a noise from above and without waiting for Doyle's reply, she darted back to see what was going on. Bodie was descending the stairs from Shelley's flat, accompanied by the forensic man who carried a large cardboard box. They both walked past Doyle and the woman without a second glance.

'Girl up there killed a copper,' she said, transferring her attention back to Doyle. 'Out at Windsor. They shot her.' The relish with which she said this was unmistakable. Doyle had found his key and was hurriedly fitting it into the lock. 'Yeah, I read about it,' he said.

'I saw her picture on telly and dialled 999,' she crowed, eager to impress. 'That's how they knew she lived here!'

Doyle opened his door. 'Good on yer, Mum,' he applauded, carrying his suitcase inside.

The woman looked at him, thoughtfully. '*She* was a student.' The implication was clear. Doyle paused to give her a massive wink, then closed the door smartly in her face.

Cowley had spent half the day at Colonel Masterson's house: talking to Frances Cottingham, going over details with Masterson. Foolproof ... Yes, it certainly looked that way. There was something, though ... something Cowley couldn't isolate and examine, that told him he was on the right track. An uneasiness about Frances? That, certainly; despite Masterson's assurances, Cowley remained suspicious of what lay beneath the cool, efficient mask she wore. More than that, however, was the fact that there were so few places the leak could have come from.

He was still worrying at the problem when he got back to his car. Bodie had arrived and was in the back seat, waiting for him. Cowley got in and sat in silence for a short time. Then, turning to Bodie, he asked: 'You like older women, don't you?'

Bodie was appalled. This case just didn't seem to be offering him a lot of scope. 'No!' he said, as forcefully as he knew how.

'That's a pity,' remarked his chief. 'I've just been talking to one I want you to take an interest in.' Avoiding the agent's look, Cowley leaned forward and signalled the driver to start moving.

The one thing no one could accuse Ray Doyle of was bad timing ... at least, not when it came to tactics in the sex war. As Shelley Hunter came downstairs from her flat, a launderette bag in her hand, he strolled out on to the landing, looking for all the world as if there was nothing else on his mind. 'Hello,' he said, affecting surprise at seeing her. 'I'm your new neighbour, my name's Ray Duncan.'

The one thing that no one could accuse Shelley Hunter of was being taken in by that sort of tactic! 'Of course it is, sweetheart,' she cooed patronisingly, and was down the stairs before he could react. Open-mouthed, he watched her go; then took the stairs to her flat two at a time, manipulated a thin oblong of celluloid between the lock and the door-frame, and was inside. The whole operation took less than twenty seconds.

He glanced round at the living-room, noticing that she'd made a cursory attempt to clean up after the forensic man, then made his way to the bathroom. Over the bath was an old-fashioned gas water-heater. Working swiftly, Doyle began to make a few simple but crucial alterations to the water-inlet system.

Bodie, meanwhile, was waiting outside Masterson's house. He'd been waiting there for what seemed a very long time. He'd read the evening paper through twice. It was not his notion of the best way to spend an evening. In fact, Bodie was fed up to the back teeth – and way beyond. Finally, Frances Cottingham left the house, got into her car and drove away. Bodie put his car into gear and followed at a sedate pace. *I wonder*, he thought, *how Doyle's getting along with that girl with the flowers on her ... jeans.*

She was carrying the launderette bag, together with a large supermarket shopping bag: swinging both; and she would have been swinging her flowers, too, if she'd been wearing those jeans. Doyle eased his door open a fraction and watched her go by. Then, as she went out of sight, he opened the door wider and poked his head out. His gaze encountered that of the witch across the landing.

'Evening,' he nodded politely.

'You're not a peeping tom, are you?' she demanded.
Doyle smiled. '*You* need have no fears, Mum.'

Bodie cut the engine and watched Frances Cottingham enter the Queen Elizabeth Hall. She was a little late for the concert and was hurrying. Bodie was in no hurry. Bodie was approaching terminal boredom. *If he's picking pansies* ... he thought viciously.

Shelley was quite naked when the heater exploded. The *boom!* was clearly audible downstairs and Doyle was out of his flat and up the stairs like lightning as the witch stared after him. He hammered at the door and in a moment Shelley appeared ... though she'd had the presence of mind to put on a wrap that covered *almost* everything. Steam and smoke were billowing out of the bathroom.

Doyle's concern was beautifully faked. 'Are you okay?' he asked, rushing into the bathroom and throwing himself at the errant heater. He shut it down and the steam began to clear. Relieved, Shelley peered over his shoulder. 'Get the Gas Board to check that,' Doyle advised. 'You could have killed yourself.'

'It's never gone wrong before.'

'Yeah, well, there's always a first time,' he said, stating the obvious.

'Right. Well. Er ... Do you know – I've quite forgotten what you said your name was.'

It wasn't quite the expression of grovelling gratitude he'd been expecting. 'Ray ...' he said, somewhat nonplussed. 'Ray Duncan.' Then he fiddled some more with the heater's controls to get an even flow of water into the bath.

'Great. Well, I hope I can do the same for you one day, Ray.'

Doyle, recovered now, saw his chance. 'Well, I was hoping you'd do something for me tonight, actually.'

'Uh-huh,' grunted Shelley; she'd heard that before somewhere.

'Yes, have dinner with me.'

She considered the offer, while she switched the hot tap off and started the cold. 'Tonight? I'm very tired; perhaps –'

'Then the hurly-burly of the great metropolis is not for you,' he suggested.

'Too right.' She was glad to have the excuse so readily accepted. Doyle had an ulterior motive, though. 'For you, O seasoned traveller,' he warbled, 'I shall prepare dishes of great delicacy to be consumed in the restful intimacy of my own humble abode.' She smiled, tempted by the jokey romanticism as much as by the pleasure of not having to cook for herself. Doyle reverted to his everyday tone to press his suit: 'I don't cook for everyone, you know. Is it a deal?'

She gave in. 'Okay, it's a deal.'

'Seven-thirty,' Doyle told her as he went off to prepare the exotic delicacies.

Cowley's car drew up by one of the roads leading in to Holland Park. He walked a few yards in towards the trees where two men were waiting. Doad was wearing a rather tatty anorak in place of the combat fatigues of the photograph; his companion was wearing a smart suit that went well with his suave good looks.

'Mr Cowley – this is Hassan Alousha, Kemel Khadi's personal assistant.' Cowley acknowledged Doad's introduction by shaking hands with the elegant young man. Then he said: 'You're ahead of schedule, Mr Doad.'

'The girl killed at Windsor,' snapped Doad. 'She was a member of the Palestinian Marxist Alliance.'

'According to her passport,' countered Cowley, 'she was Spanish.'

'Her nationality doesn't matter. What matters is that she was PMA.' Doad insisted; Alousha underlined the point by adding: 'A faction violently opposed to Kemel Khadi.'

Doad said what they all knew to be true: 'Khadi will

now be in great danger while in England.'

Cowley considered the implications. 'We shall ensure his safety, Mr Doad. You have no cause for alarm.'

Doad scoffed. 'I think I have every cause for alarm. That girl was here for a reason ... to gain intelligence. Yet Kemel Khadi's visit and his itinerary were known only to Alousha and myself – and to your people. There was no leak at our end.'

Cowley stood firm. 'I can only repeat, Mr Doad, that Kemel Khadi will be quite safe while under my protection.'

'You must excuse me,' said Doad, equally firmly. 'In the circumstances I'm afraid I must take my own measures to ensure Kemel Khadi's safety.'

'Which will be?' Cowley wanted to know.

'They'll be efficient, Mr Cowley.'

'We cannot permit agents of any foreign power to carry weapons in this country.'

'Try telling that to the PMA,' said Doad harshly.

Cowley was adamant. 'If you attempt to mount your own security operation, the consequences might prove extremely embarrassing – both to us and to you.'

'More so than Kemel Khadi cancelling his visit at the last minute?' Doad's question was rhetorical. He knew – Cowley knew – that Khadi's visit could solve many problems. A cancellation was unthinkable.

'I *am* glad that you found it all right.' Doyle leaned on the door jamb and regarded Shelley, who was looking, if anything, prettier and more seductive than she had in her bath-wrap.

'Got a sense of direction second to none,' she smiled as she took in the table laid for two and the subdued lighting.

'I thought the Captain worried about all that,' said Doyle, miming a parody of a chronically short-sighted pilot.

'Mostly, I worry about the Captain.'

'Mind not on the job?'

'Mind not on flying,' she answered and gave him a slow smile. *Promising,* thought Doyle, *distinctly promising.*

Bodie leaned on a railing and looked down at the murky water of the Thames. A tiny flotilla of debris washed to and fro: a flattened cardboard box, three polystyrene cups, a plank with a cluster of rusty nails driven in – it slopped against the wall and the pattern changed: the cups overtook the plank, the box lost contact with the rest, Bodie lost his bet with himself ... Sighing, he turned and rested his elbows on the rail and looked towards the concert hall. A seepage of music came to him along the walkway. It seemed likely to go on for ever. Bodie began to feel hungry.

Shelley wound spaghetti round her fork and manoeuvred it to her mouth, chewing appreciatively before answering Doyle's question. 'We were only in the flat together for one night. She seemed homesick. Talked about her folks and her kid brother.'

'Next day,' observed Doyle, thrusting his own fork into the pasta, 'she goes out and shoots down a nice old cop in cold blood.'

Shelley didn't seem too taken aback by the idea. 'Yeah,' she said, 'you never can tell.' She took another forkful, then said, 'Hey!' sharply.

Doyle's head jerked up. 'This is a pretty mean spaghetti bolognese,' she grinned.

Doyle gave his well-known impression of an Italian waiter: 'We aim-a to pleez ... !'

Mozart, thought Bodie, *definitely Mozart*; then he checked his watch, wondering whether his stamina was greater than that of Wolfgang Amadeus. He looked up to see Frances Cottingham leaving the hall and grimaced with relief. As he followed her towards the car park, he passed a poster advertising the performance of Beethoven string quartets. Bodie lost a second bet with himself. He hoped fervently that Doyle was spending a boring evening too.

'I know this little club,' Ray Doyle offered, 'but a light year from Leicester Square ...'

Shelley reached over and took his hand. 'Ray, thanks – but it's been a long day.' He smiled, accepting defeat it seemed. 'Would you mind?' she asked.

'Of course not.'

She stood up. 'It's been a great evening, Ray.'

'It's been a very short one,' he checked his watch. 'It's only nine o'clock.'

'I'm flying at six,' she protested.

Doyle moved over and put his mouth next to her ear. 'Doesn't it make your arms sore?' he whispered; then he drew her close and kissed her lingeringly.

'I've got a very high pain threshold,' she whispered back, making no move to escape.

His arms tightened round her waist. 'Is that what it's called?'

Frances Cottingham went straight to the apartment block where she lived: no interesting diversions, no mysterious stops en route. Bodie sat in his car staring moodily at the entrance to the block, then he picked up his R/T. '3.7 ... 3.7.'

'Where are you 3.7?' – Cowley's voice on the other end.

'Outside target's house.'

'What do you think?'

In a voice laden with feeling, Bodie said, 'I think maybe I should have stayed in the army!'

The room was in almost total darkness – just a few needle-thin lines of dawn light filtering through the curtains; and there was silence – apart from the faint, muted bumping coming from overhead. Doyle had been awake for a minute or so, listening. He reached over and laid a hand on the smooth, tanned curve of Shelley's shoulder, joggling her till she woke and looked at him in confusion.

'You don't have a very large cat up there, do you?'

'Wha –'

'You don't have a large domestic pet in your flat?'

She looked at him as if he'd gone mad. 'What're you talking about?'

A just-audible scraping noise came from above their heads. 'That,' he replied.

The two men in Shelley's flat weren't being too tidy; but they were being thorough. The place was ransacked: clothes, books, papers, bric-à-brac were tumbled about the place. One man had been working the sitting-room, while the other turned the bedroom over. Now, they came together, one shaking his head at the other to indicate: *Nothing!* As they moved towards the front door of the flat, Doyle cleared the last stair and reached the door on the other side. It moved slightly as he reached for the knob. Taking a step backwards, Doyle hurled himself at it, slamming into the man on the far side, who cannoned back into his partner. Doyle stepped through and in the same motion hit the man who was standing hard in the mouth; he dropped and Doyle turned to aim a kick at the figure on the floor. He found himself looking down the barrel of a silenced revolver.

The second man waved the gun jerkily: telling Doyle to get out of the way of the door. Then he heard footsteps ascending the stair. *Back-up!* Doyle could see the thought going through the man's head as the footsteps came closer. He lunged across Doyle to slam the door – and as he did so, Doyle chopped at the hand holding the gun, catching the nerve just behind the wristbone. The gun fell on to the floor as Doyle grappled with the intruder.

The second man was up on one knee, his own gun

out, trying to get a clear shot at Doyle – who obligingly threw his opponent clear, attempting to get a punch in. Doyle's head came into the sights – just as Shelley pushed in through the door, sending him reeling. The bullet splintered the woodwork; then both intruders were running back into the living-room.

Shelley was frozen with fear. Then she looked at the bullet hole in the panel by her head and said, 'Oh my God!' Doyle grabbed the gun from the carpet and set off in pursuit, stumbling through the mess in the living-room and shouldering his way into the kitchen as another shot – high and wide – chipped the door-frame. The men were clambering through a skylight, one of them keeping Doyle pinned down, while the other hoisted himself up. When he was sure that they were both through and on to the roof, Doyle swung up after them.

They'd covered twenty yards or so, scrambling over sloping roofs and sliding into the gulleys between, sending tiles spinning and slithering in their wake. They'd gone another ten yards or so, when one man slipped as a line of tiles came adrift beneath his feet. It was enough for Doyle. His flying tackle dragged his quarry further down and they rolled together, a flurry of limbs, to the edge of the parapet. Doyle ducked the knee that whistled towards his face, so that his attacker's leg scythed upwards on the follow-through. The violence of the action took the man off-balance. He staggered, his foot stamping, as if in anger, on the very last row of tiles as he fought to stay upright; then he was gone with a shrill cry as he fell, arching outwards, into the deserted street below.

Shelley turned in alarm as she heard the noise at the skylight; her face relaxed, though, when she saw it was Doyle lowering himself back into the kitchen.

'Are you okay?' she asked anxiously. Then, 'Where are they?'

'One got away over the roofs,' replied Doyle, panting.

'What about the other?'

'He – er – took the quick way down.' He crossed to the telephone and Shelley looked alarmed.

'You're not going to call the cops, are you?'

'I don't know whether you noticed,' he said sardonically, 'but those guys were armed.'

'Yeah –' she tried a joke, '– gets more like New York every day.' She looked serious, though, as she walked across to where Doyle stood, holding the phone.

'Look, Ray, the cops are already on to me about that kamikaze kid disguised as a fiddle player. If they get in on tonight . . . ker-boom!'

'We don't have guilt by association in this country,' he told her. 'Not yet, anyway.'

'Ah, come on Ray, you know the score,' she pleaded. 'The cops can make it clear to my employers that I'm no longer welcome here without giving any reason.'

'And your employers,' he replied reasonably, 'can tell them to get lost.'

'They could, but they won't. I'm out of a job, out of the country and out of luck.' She looked winsome. 'I like it here.'

'Despite the fact that it's getting more and more like New York?'

'Despite that!' she exclaimed.

Doyle looked at her a moment, then dialled 999. She returned the look with one of her own that clearly spelled 'Bastard!' then her features softened as she heard him say: 'Ambulance.' There was a tiny delay before he continued: 'Oldham Gardens . . . No number. He's outside . . . Don't worry, you can't miss him.' Then he hung up.

'Like I said: we get burglaries around here.' Shelley was offering an explanation.

'Like you said to whom?'

'Some cop who was in here yesterday.'

Doyle did his best to look intrigued. 'That mean-looking character I saw coming down the stairs?'

'I thought he was rather cute.' She could tease, now

that her fear of facing another question-answer session was gone.

'I didn't like the look of him,' Doyle said. 'I shouldn't let him in if he comes back – you can't be too careful these days.'

'I can look after myself.'

Doyle grinned at her. 'The kind of visitors you get –' he looked round expressively at her jumbled belongings, '– you'd need to.'

She smiled her agreement. 'How fortunate that I had a man about the place ... What did you say you do?'

'Student.'

'What are you majoring in,' she wanted to know, 'counter-insurgency?' From the scattered tins and packets in the kitchen, she salvaged some coffee, then filled the kettle with water and set it on the stove.

'I used to be in the Marines,' said Doyle eventually.

She put a couple of mugs on the work surface. 'I bet they were sorry when you left,' she chuckled. Then, with a nice sense of the ridiculous, she added, 'Do you take sugar?'

Bodie might have been cute the previous day; but slumped in the seat of his car, wearing the previous day's clothes and showing a dark, half-mask of stubble, he looked and felt as far from being cute as an irate grizzly. Rubbing his eyes and stretching his cramped legs, he reflected that there were almost certainly more entertaining ways of passing the time. *Why this?* he thought. *I could have been a filing clerk, or a greengrocer, or a park attendant – jobs filled with action and endless interest. I could have had an assembly-line job, or ...* His speculations ended as Frances Cottingham came out of the house, being towed along by a large dog and heading in the direction of the park. Wearily, Bodie reached for the door handle. 'I *should* have stayed in the army,' he muttered.

*

Ray Doyle scratched at his unshaven chin as he came downstairs from Shelley's flat. Unlike Bodie, he was smiling. He reached his landing to find the old woman from across the hall peering at him from her door. In a very knowing voice, she said, 'Morning.'

Doyle wasn't to be chastened. 'Morning, Mum,' he replied cheerily as he let himself into his flat. It came as no surprise to him to find Cowley seated in the only comfortable chair, reading the morning paper.

'Heard the news this morning, or were you too busy?' Cowley's tone matched that of the old woman.

'Er – no – I mean, yes, I was.' This time Doyle had the good grace to blush slightly before recovering himself to offer an explanation that came straight from the heart: 'She was *very* upset.'

Cowley sounded unconvinced. 'The Mona Lisa opposite put a different interpretation on your actions,' he said in a droll tone.

'Wait till I get the rotor arm out of her broomstick.'

'Just don't take it out on the black cat,' remarked Cowley, joining in the banter, 'I'm a life member of the RSPCA.' His voice changed: 'I take it the sky-diver attempted entry?'

'Two of them did. Took nothing.' Doyle lifted his head, indicating that his next remark concerned Shelley. 'She wouldn't call the police. Says she's worried about her work permit.'

Cowley got up from the chair and wandered over to the window. 'I heard her leave a little while back.'

'Yeah, Cairo,' Doyle informed him. Then, trying to read his Chief's mind, added: 'Shall I get her back?'

'No need.' Cowley smiled crookedly, 'I've already lined up another one for you. You'll like this one. She's interested in music!'

'I thought she was down to Bodie!' Doyle sounded almost plaintive.

'Not any more,' came the amused reply.

Chapter Thirteen

The hospital smell assaulted Bodie's nostrils as he made his way towards the side-ward in the Intensive Care Unit; a smell of ether and polish and disinfectant – and something else, something indefinable that bound the other odours, but was stronger than all of them. The smell of decay, perhaps, of sickness. The accumulated, lingering, sordid fragrance of a million dying breaths. Bodie hated it; deep down, maybe, he feared it. Lengthening his stride, he reached the side-ward and walked in among the forest of drip-stanchions, sensors and oxygen cannisters. A doctor was attending to the man who had fallen from the roof during the fight with Doyle.

Bodie said nothing: he merely raised his eyebrows. The doctor replied in kind, shrugging. The shrug meant: 'I don't know ... probably not.' Bodie watched the plasma drip releasing its fluid like a leaky tap; his eyes dropped towards the unconscious man on the bed; finally, he looked around at the life-support systems by the bed. *Better*, he thought, *much better a clean kill.*

Doyle wedged the cap down on his mop of curls as he walked out of the lift and approached the door of Frances Cottingham's flat. He was dressed in the uniform of a Gas Board official and carried an impressive-looking ring-file. He tried to look the part. The baggy trousers and shapeless jacket helped, but the cap sat on top of his head like a lid that hasn't been screwed down.

He rang the doorbell and after a few seconds the door was opened a few inches, checking as the security chain caught. Mrs Cottingham – Frances's mother – peered through the gap. For one insane moment, Doyle thought the old lady was on her knees; then he realised she was seated in a motorised wheelchair.

'Er – Gas Board, Ma'am.' He adopted what he hoped was a convincing voice for a meter-reader.

'Well?'

'Come to read the meter,' he said lamely.

'You only came last week.' He hadn't been prepared for this. 'No I never,' he said, sounding almost petulant.

'Someone did,' insisted the old lady.

Doyle improvised wildly. 'Yeah ... well ... he got run over, see. Er – the whole street's got to be done again.'

Mrs Cottingham thought this over for a minute and seemed to find it reasonable. She slid the chain back and let Doyle in. He stood in the hallway, looking round rather vaguely while she watched suspiciously. Eventually she said, 'The cupboard – over there.'

'Yeah – of course!' Doyle hurried towards it, found the meter and went through a charade of note-taking. Next he emerged and made for the kitchen. 'Just check the appliances ...'

Mrs Cottingham pressed a button on the arm of her wheelchair and advanced a few feet towards him. 'They've never done that before,' she observed, watching him closely.

'Yeah ... well ... we're trying to improve the service all the time.' He fled into the small kitchen and made a show of examining the gas stove. The wheelchair whirred up behind him, blocking the door. 'North Sea gas,' he said trying to appear knowledgeable. 'Expect it gives you a lot of problems.'

'None at all,' said the old lady, surprised. Doyle continued to peer at the cooker as if expecting it to speak his weight or suddenly change colour.

Bodie watched the man breathe in, then out, then shakily in – an act that had seemed to become, for this person at least, terrifyingly tenuous. The life support apparatus blipped and dripped; a screen glowing dimly green registered a hesitant heartbeat.

Cowley entered the side-ward and stood behind Bodie. 'How is he?' The sentence sounded harshly in the quiet room. 'No change,' said Bodie, not looking up.

'Anything on him?'

'Not a light,' replied the agent. 'Have ballistics come back about the gun?'

'Yes: the serial was filed off.' As he spoke, Cowley handed Bodie a midday edition of the evening paper. It bore the headline: GUNMAN FALLS FROM ROOF, followed by a sub-head that read: *Expected to live.* Bodie glanced at it, then at Cowley. 'So his brothers in arms know where he is?' He'd noticed that the name of the hospital was given in the story.

'And they'll think he can still talk,' amplified Cowley. *Live bait,* thought Bodie looking down at the unconscious man. *But for how long?*

'Right!' said Ray Doyle in a business-like manner, getting up from his knees. He'd spent as much time on the cooker as he dared . . . and still Mrs Cottingham watched him like a hawk.

'Young man,' she said waspishly, 'if your purpose in coming here is to sell me a new gas oven, you may forget it. My daughter and I find this one perfectly adequate for our needs.'

Doyle affected interest. 'Oh, you live with your daughter, do you?' He was beginning to think she'd never leave him alone: at which moment the phone rang. Mrs Cottingham swung the chair in a tight circle and took it at full throttle into the hall. 'Hello . . . Oh, Frances, yes dear . . .' Doyle waited until the conversation had begun, then ducked into the bathroom. A quick look round there and on to the sitting-room, as Mrs Cottingham was saying, '. . . but you did say you'd be home early tonight.'

'Won't be a tick,' Doyle assured her as he went into the main room. She leaned back in an effort to see what he was doing and the telephone crashed to the floor. 'I'm sorry dear,' she said into the mouthpiece, '... it's this man ...'

Doyle was investigating a large hi-fi unit flanked by shelf after shelf of records; he had a 'bug' concealed in his hand and was looking for a place to fix it when Mrs Cottingham came into the room at top speed. 'Leave that alone!' she ordered.

'Beautiful isn't it,' said Doyle, backing away. 'I love good music.'

The old lady was beginning to sound a little hysterical. 'My daughter is waiting on the phone. If you do not leave immediately, she will call the police.'

'Don't worry, missus – just off.' She retreated to the phone and picked up the handset. 'It's all right, Frances. He's going ... Very well, dear, I'll expect you at seven ...'

Doyle closed the door. The bug was clenched in his hand!

It was a good thing, he reflected later, that CI5 had other resources. If everything had depended on his placing the bug, he might have been on the receiving end of some pretty scathing words from Cowley. As it was, both he and his boss were on the receiving end of a telephone intercept device, installed in the back of a GPO van that stood outside the Cottinghams' apartment, suitably camouflaged by an inspection tent standing over a junction box in the street. There had been a few insignificant calls before they got what they were waiting for.

'You did say you had someone for tonight.' It was Frances Cottingham's voice.

'But you never made a firm booking, Miss Cottingham.' The person on the other end of the line sounded genuinely apologetic; Frances sounded a touch frantic. 'You claim to offer a twenty-four-hour nursing service,' she complained.

'That's right; and we need twenty-four hours' notice. I am sorry.' Frances hung up; the receiver in the GPO van went dead.

'Pity about the bug,' Cowley said mildly.

Doyle was anxious to make little of it. 'Yeah, well, there you go,' he said ruefully.

'Quite.' Cowley's glance was decidedly wry; but before he could add anything, the sound of dialling came through on the receiver, followed by a ringing tone. No one answered. Frances Cottingham let it ring and ring.

'She's not having too much luck tonight is she?' Doyle observed.

'Not the only one,' replied his chief.

'Hope springs eternal,' offered Doyle, turning to a small scanner screen and making a few adjustments to the bank of switches on the control unit. The number Frances had dialled came up on the screen and Doyle snapped on his hand R/T. '4.5 to base ... 4.5 to base, over.' The ringing tone continued. 'Come on Alex, come on,' Doyle muttered. Again he tried: '4.5 to base ... Over!'

'Base to 4.5. Go ahead.'

'Alex, we want a trace on a phone number: 875 4066.'

'Will do 4.5. Don't go away. Over.'

As Doyle broke radio contact, the ringing tone ceased and a voice said, ' 'Allo?'

'Luis?' Frances's voice was breathless with anxiety.

'*Querida,*' came the reply.

'I thought you'd never answer.'

'There was difficulties.' The man was being non-committal.

'I must see you – tonight.'

'Tonight – I cannot.'

'Luis, I think we're being watched.'

'Watched? What do you mean?'

'A man was at the apartment. He said he was from the gas board, but Mother thinks he was snooping. A nasty piece of work, she says.'

Cowley looked at Doyle, who tried not to catch his eye.

'Tomorrow evening, as arranged,' said the man abruptly and hung up.

Doyle's R/T bleeped. A voice said: '4.5? Please acknowledge 4.5.'

Doyle pressed the switch. 'Yeah, Alex, what've you got?'

'A phone box. At Waterloo Station main entrance, would you believe?'

'Thanks, Alex. Out.' Bodie put down the R/T and looked at Cowley. 'Shall we bring her in?'

Cowley shook his head. 'After I've spoken to Masterson.'

A-squad's chief liked to observe the proprieties.

Bodie's back-up team had spotted them before they'd got as far as the Intensive Care Unit – Doad, in the garb of a House Surgeon, Alousha and the man who had escaped Doyle that morning dressed as theatre staff. As part of the subterfuge they were pushing a trolley, coming through the swing doors at the end of the dim corridor leading to the side-ward. They'd covered half the distance, when the lights went up and Bodie, along with another CI5 man, stepped into the open, their guns drawn.

'Freeze!' Bodie said it quietly, but very distinctly. The three men did just that; then the door to the Unit kitchen opened and a nurse stepped into the corridor and saw – or thought she saw – three members of hospital staff being held at gunpoint by two men. 'What the ... ?' She gasped, her hand going to her mouth. It was just enough of a distraction. Doad shoved the trolley at Bodie, then turned and sprinted back down the corridor followed by the other two impostors. Bodie stiff-armed the trolley to one side and gave chase.

Beyond the double-doors was a staircase giving access to an upper floor and to the basement. Alousha, with the third man following, took the flight leading up; Doad plunged downwards, taking the steps three at a time. Bodie peeled off after Doad, leaving the CI5 man to pursue the others. The stairs down led to a series of service tunnels and Bodie could hear Doad's running footfalls echoing in the enclosed space; then they stopped. Bodie pulled up after he'd covered another fifty feet or so and looked round. To his left was a cavernous boiler-room, the door ajar. He walked in, slammed the door loudly and threw the bar into its 'lock' position.

'You're trapped,' he shouted. 'Why not make it easy for both of us.' There was no noise but the hiss of steam. Bodie sidled past one of the great cylinders, then heard the dull 'clunk' of something knocking against it on the other side. He rounded the boiler to find Doad attempting to scale an inspection ladder that led to a metal trapdoor in the roof. Gun raised, Bodie spoke in a level, pleasant voice: 'There's the easy way and there's the hard way. You choose.'

Doad descended the ladder, his face expressionless, and raised his hands.

'Well, well,' said Bodie mockingly, 'Aziz Doad – may his tribe increase.'

Old techniques are the best – Cowley knew that. They're the best because people don't change: their reactions, their fears, their weaknesses don't change. Catch them when they're unprepared, at their lowest ebb; keep the element of surprise; catch them at a time when you're alert and they're not, when you are in command and they are disadvantaged. Catch them, if you can, with their trousers down. It was Cowley's theory – and that's why he and Doyle rang Frances Cottingham's front door bell at 5.30 a.m. the next morning.

She opened the door in a robe, looking sleepy and puzzled. Cowley was brisk: 'Do you mind if we come in, Miss Cottingham?'

'Mr Cowley, it's five-thirty in the morning.'

'Having been up all night,' retorted Cowley, 'I'm only too aware of the time.'

She kept them standing in the hall. 'Can't whatever it is wait?'

'I'm afraid not,' he said. 'I do have to talk to you now.'

She slipped the chain off and admitted them. Mrs Cottingham's voice, sounding anxious, came from a bedroom. 'Frances? Frances! What is it?'

'Now you've woken Mother.' Frances looked flustered.

'Frances!' the old lady called querulously, 'Who is it? It's five-thirty a.m.!'

Shooting Cowley and Doyle murderous glances, she hurried into her mother's room where the old lady was sitting up in bed, looking frightened and indignant at the same time. 'What *is* going on, Frances?' she demanded.

'It's all right Mother. Just colleagues of Colonel Masterson.'

'At five-thirty? It really is too bad!'

'Urgent business.' Frances patted the pillow by her mother's head and tugged at the blankets. 'You try to get back to sleep.'

She entered the living-room to find Doyle and Cowley standing by the hi-fi equipment. Cowley regarded her sternly. 'Shut the door, Miss Cottingham. I've no wish to upset your mother,' She hesitated, watching his face, then did as she'd been told. When the door was secure, Cowley switched on the tape-deck attached to the hi-fi and the spools began to turn.

''Allo?'

'Luis?'

'*Querida.*'

'I thought you'd never answer.'

'There was difficulties.'

'I must see you – tonight.'

'Tonight – I cannot.'

'Luis, I think we are being watched!'

Throughout the tape, Frances Cottingham's face remained frozen. She showed no surprise, nor did she look at either man. Her eyes were fixed on the tape as it glided over the machine-head; even when the recording finished, she continued to stare stonily at it.

Cowley switched off. 'Well, Miss Cottingham?'

She looked up as if seeing him for the first time. 'It's not a crime to have an affair – even with a younger man, is it?' she asked at length.

'If it isn't, why were you worried about being watched?'

'His wife was jealous,' she spoke without emotion. 'Luis feared she had put a private detective on to him.'

'Luis was dependant on his wife for money?' Cowley wanted to know.

'Only for his work. That's not a crime either.'

Cowley decided that the time for fencing was over. 'But making your lover privy to highly confidential information concerning your employer's business affairs is,' he observed coldly. 'Particularly when those affairs are affairs of state.'

'Luis isn't interested in affairs of state, confidential or otherwise. He's a musician.'

Cowley pressed his point: 'Then why did you tell him about Kemel Khadi?'

'I didn't! You've absolutely no proof.'

Cowley held up the tape that he'd taken from the deck. 'I have the voice of a very frightened man.'

'Persecuted by a jealous wife!'

Cowley took issue with that. 'Persecuted? But you say she has supported him during his infidelity. Surely she can't have known?'

'She found out,' countered Frances. 'Luis thought she had found out.'

Cowley studied her for a moment. 'Miss Cottingham,' he began, 'I know you a lot better than you think.'

'How can someone like you possibly know me?' – there was anger in her voice.

'I know you're forty-five years old; that for most of your life, music's been your only real love.'

'So you've talked to Colonel Masterson.' She was scornful. 'Congratulations Mr Cowley; how acute you are!'

Pausing slightly to make the words tell, Cowley asked: 'Have you had many lovers, Miss Cottingham?'

The scorn turned to outrage. 'I *beg* your pardon?'

'Luis *was* important to you?' Cowley clarified.

'He *is* important.'

'To both of us,' he agreed. 'Because what I don't yet know is: who is Luis Delgado working for?'

Without its paraphernalia of drips and monitor screens and respirators, the side-ward looked strangely bare. Bodie and Doad watched as a nurse wheeled out the last of the equipment that had kept the patient alive. The man looked no different in death than he had before the last blip had faltered across the screen, before the last intake of breath. Now, though, something was missing; something that had wavered, fought, but then finally accepted defeat. Bodie imagined that last, noxious breath mingling with the air.

Cowley entered the ward and Bodie walked over to him. 'They certified him dead about twenty minutes ago,' he said. His chief nodded, then lowered his voice to ask: 'What about the two with Doad?'

'Jameson nabbed one of 'em. The other got away.'

Cowley frowned and walked across to Doad. 'I'm sorry, Doad,' – his voice conveyed anything but sorrow – 'I did warn you to leave it to us.'

'Kemel Khadi's visit is now out of the question,' was his response.

'Because one of your men has died from injuries received while committing a crime?'

Doad's tone sharpened: 'I'm not interested in the niceties of British criminal law, Mr Cowley. My concern is to keep Kemel Khadi alive. If my men have to burglarise to do it – then so be it.'

'If you'd asked me, I would have told you what we found in the girl's flat: nothing.' Cowley was no less biting.

'I told you, Cowley – I prefer to work independently. Particularly as your security is leaking so badly.'

'The leak's been plugged!' It was Cowley's trump card

and it had the desired effect: Doad registered first surprise, then relief. 'Perhaps you'd like to meet her?' continued Cowley. The baffled look on Doad's face afforded him particular pleasure.

Masterson, Cowley, Doyle, Bodie, Doad – Frances Cottingham faced all five men apprehensively, the whiteness of her knuckles betraying the tension she felt. In her small office – her domain – she no longer maintained any control.

'Luis Delgado!' – Cowley was attacking, sure of his ground.

'Why must this go on?' pleaded Frances 'I've told you all I know.'

'Are you sure, Miss Cottingham? You see it's no longer just a question of who Luis Delgado is working for and how much you told him. It's a question of who *is* Luis Delgado?'

'I've *told* you!' she insisted.

'But what you've told us doesn't check out.'

Alarm spread over the woman's face. 'You haven't spoken to his wife?'

'Unfortunately not,' said Cowley. He registered her relief, then turned to Doyle – second wave of the attack.

'No one of that name lives in Burleigh Mansions.' Doyle rapped out the information. 'Neither does any young musician – Spanish or otherwise, with or without a rich wife. No Luis Delgado was ever enrolled as a postgraduate student of the Royal College of Music, or the Madrid Conservatoire.'

'In fact,' Cowley delivered the *coup de grâce*, 'nothing you claim Luis told you about himself stands up to enquiry.'

'I don't believe you!' It was said out of bravado; from her tremulous tone, it was clear that she did believe – or was beginning to.

'I am afraid it's true, Frances.' This from Masterson: the final blow. She opened her mouth to speak, her lips working, but emitting no sound; her eyes darkened with fear and anguish. Her hands unlocked and began to tremble uncontrollably. Cowley stopped the attack, adopting the pose of the compassionate victor. 'Miss Cottingham,' he said softly, 'you have been the victim of an elaborate confidence trick, the sole purpose of which was to elicit from you intelligence about Colonel Masterson's relationship with Kemel Khadi.'

Frances Cottingham's face contorted: there were no tears, no sound to express her pain; but her mouth opened and her eyes grew wide, giving her the appearance of someone who has just witnessed a terrible sight, or has stepped out into space, suddenly, shockingly, when she expected to feel firm ground beneath her feet.

Slowly, infinitely slowly, her features came together again; but the pain remained. 'All right –' her voice was surprisingly steady. 'I told him. I didn't mean to. But I told him.' Ignoring the others, she looked directly at Masterson. 'I'm so sorry.'

For a long moment, there was silence. Cowley broke it, looking at Doad and asking: 'A word?' Doad nodded and the two men left the room, followed by Doyle. All three walked out into the garden, Doyle peeling off towards his car. Cowley stopped him. 'Have you vacated your temporary abode?' he wanted to know.

'Not yet,' replied Doyle, 'why?'

'I think it's time you gave the taxpayers a break.'

Doyle didn't answer: just made a move towards the car. Cowley stopped him again: 'Oh, and Doyle . . .' The agent paused and looked over his shoulder. '. . . Try and fit in a shave,' said his chief, then turned quickly back to Doad before he could take the full force of Doyle's glare.

'As we've isolated the leak,' he argued, watching Doad's face for a reaction, 'all we have to do now is to change the rendezvous and Khadi's visit can go ahead. Agreed?'

'Providing the meeting does not take place as scheduled – in Mayfair – yes.'

'I've already spoken to the FO and they've made a country house available. The meeting will take place under my personal supervision.'

'Agreed – providing the PMA in Mayfair are placed under *my* personal supervision!'

Cowley could see that one coming. His answer was short and to the point: 'No!'

'Yes!' Doad was every bit as insistent. 'If you want Kemel Khadi's visit to go ahead.'

'Mayfair is too rich in innocent bystanders.' Cowley dug his heels in; but he reserved the right to give a little ground eventually – enough to make Doad think he'd won a victory.

'Rich being the operative word?'

Cowley countered the sneer: 'Rich, innocent and influential being the operative words.'

'So these PMA animals live on to kill more people? I'm fighting a war, Mr Cowley.'

'The war will go on,' Cowley assured him, 'but not in Mayfair.'

Doad's lip curled. 'No doubt Salisbury Plain would be more convenient for you; but how are you going to convince the PMA of that?'

Cowley turned, as Masterson joined them in the garden, and looked directly at the window of Frances Cottingham's study; she sat, as they had left her, in her office chair, her head bowed.

'You can't rely on that woman,' exclaimed Doad, understanding immediately what Cowley's plan was. 'She's finished.'

'Possibly. But what have we got to lose? The opposition are on a hiding to nothing.'

'A what?' The expression meant nothing to Doad.

'If Miss Cottingham is believed,' Cowley explained, 'then the terrorists will come where they can be dealt with. If she is not believed, then they still won't know where Mr Khadi is going – and will be able to do nothing.'

'And what about Frances?' Masterson asked pertinently.

This time Cowley didn't give an inch. 'If the Khadi visit is as vital to British interests as you claim, I don't think we have any choice, Colonel. Do you?'

Back in her office, Cowley tried to pitch his tone somewhere between the stern and the avuncular. 'How do you feel now, Miss Cottingham?' he asked.

She looked up wearily. 'I don't know. Confused.'

'I think you must accept that you have been very foolish.'

'Yes.' There was a wealth of feeling in the single word.

'You have betrayed not only your employer,' went on Cowley, 'but also your country.'

'Mr Cowley,' there was a kind of desperate anger in her voice: an anger directed at herself, 'I'm very ashamed. I admit I have been very foolish; but what else can I do? I've told you where I arranged to meet the man I knew as Luis. If you want to know his real identity – who he's really working for – then you'll have to ask him yourself. *I don't know.*'

Cowley turned to Masterson and raised an eyebrow. The Colonel played his part: 'Frances,' he said gently, 'it is possible for you to retrieve the situation.'

'What do you mean?' Anxiety crept back into her voice.

Cowley took over: 'Keep your meeting with Luis Delgado this evening.'

'What on earth for?'

He produced a card from his pocket. 'Luis will want to know where Khadi is going to stay.' He proffered the card. 'This is the address you are to give him.'

'The Crableigh Hotel ...' she read it out loud, still not quite sure what was being proposed.

'A remote spot in the country,' Cowley informed her, 'largely used by anglers in-season. The owner used to be in MI6.'

She saw, now, what they were asking of her. To see Luis again, to suffer the pain of facing him and knowing he had used her – gained her love – but cared nothing for her. To touch him, to be touched ... to lie in his arms and listen to his deceits, his empty promises. It hurt; it hurt more than words could express. She looked up at Cowley, then at Masterson. Her voice was unsteady. 'I don't know that I can bring myself to do it ...' her gaze fell away and she coloured. '... Physically, I mean.' None of the men spoke. Frances looked up once more and met Cowley's eyes. 'I'll try,' she said firmly.

Chapter Fourteen

Sleep, thought Ray Doyle, *that's what I could do with: a few hours' kip*. His eyes felt gritty and there was a weariness in his limbs. Then he recollected the reasons for his lack of sleep and smiled as he trudged up the stairs to his temporary flat, toting milk and bread in a carrier-bag. The old witch was waving a scuffed broom at the muckier corners of the landing.

'Got to make an effort, haven't you?' She looked at Doyle accusingly – maybe it was *his* turn to sweep.

'Admirable sentiments, Mum,' he agreed, fumbling for his key. Before he could let himself in, his attention was taken by a man coming upstairs. Slim, good-looking, dark-complexion ... Doyle had never seen Alousha before, so he registered nothing but the guy's physical characteristics – and the fact that he was going up to Shelley's door. He watched as the stranger produced a key and let himself in to Shelley's flat; then he turned to his nosey neighbour, who was watching him with spiteful glee. 'Didn't think you were the only one, did you?' she gloated.

'He been here before?' Doyle wanted to get it straight.

'Oh yeah, not 'alf,' she chuckled delightedly. Doyle nodded, then slammed his own door behind him.

'They used to be like that with me once,' said the crone, to no one in particular. 'Like bees round a honey pot.' Moodily, she rattled the brush around the skirting board, before retreating to her lonely room and the cat.

When Alousha finally left Shelley's flat, he found Doyle waiting for him: lounging against his door jamb and watching as Alousha came downstairs. The two men regarded each other for a moment. Then Doyle said: 'Friend of Shelley's are you?'

The effect was electric. Alousha moved so fast – and so unexpectedly – that Doyle was left gaping for a full five seconds. Then he bolted after the man, following him round to the back of the house. A wall at the bottom of the garden divided patches of green and ran out to a main road. Alousha leapt on to the brickwork just as Doyle raced up to him and made a grab for his legs. Alousha kicked out, catching the agent on the side of the head and sending him spinning. Red lightning flashes shot through Doyle's brain; the blackness of tunnel vision started to crowd in on him. Then he shook his head and, still shaky, hoisted himself on to the wall and gave chase.

Alousha was approaching the junction where the wall met the road; but he knew that Doyle was gaining on him. He stopped, found a firm balance, then produced a gun and fired at virtually point-blank range. Doyle had seen it coming – the man wasn't stopping to pass the time of day, he knew that! He was moving sideways before the first crash of the .38 rang in his ears: leaping from the wall and out of the line of fire. Alousha pocketed the gun and jumped down into the roadway. Doyle lay amid the splintered wreckage of a small greenhouse. He sat up, feeling stupid, and dabbed at a cut on his chin.

By the time he got back to his landing, there was blood on his shirt and hands. He regarded it ruefully. His neighbour was making a pretence of looking for her cat. 'Mojo! Mojo! she called; then, betraying the real reason for her appearance on the landing, asked: 'Did you catch him, then?'

Doyle shook his head, then looked up at Shelley's door. 'She's still not back, dear,' she said with a sly smile. Then, as he walked through into his flat, she called out, 'They do say absence makes the heart grow fonder.'

'Do they just?' Doyle injected venom into the question and banged the door to.

The hotel was neither smart nor seedy – neither expensive nor down at heel; it was, if anything, anonymous. In its plain, unadorned rooms people spent time out of time: its discreetly curtained windows displayed nothing of the boredom of the lonely one-night guest, nothing of the lust or anguish or temporary affection of those who made use of the rooms for an afternoon or a couple of hours; nothing of the lies that were told ... or the secrets.

From their car, parked unobtrusively in a side-street, Cowley and Bodie watched Frances Cottingham enter the hotel. 'Take your seats, please,' Bodie's voice was cynical, 'tonight's performance is about to begin.'

'Let's just hope it's an award winner,' his chief remarked. 'Afterwards – you tail him. Doyle can look after her.'

'If Doyle ever gets here.'

Cowley checked his watch. 'It shouldn't take him all night to have a wash and shave,' he said grumpily.

Bodie grinned impishly: 'But there may be distractions!'

Before Cowley could take him up on this, Bodie nodded towards the street. 'Ah, behold: Luis the Latin lover.' They saw Luis leave his car and go into the hotel.

'If music be the food of love ...' began Cowley.

'... play on,' boomed Bodie, 'play on!' Without taking his eyes from the window of the room Frances Cottingham had booked, he picked up his R/T. '4.5? 4.5? Come in.' A crackle of static was his only reply. '4.5: whatever you're doing, stop it and report back!' Still nothing. Bodie reflected that it seemed to be his lot, just lately, to sit in a car, watching and listening, while others had all the fun.

'If Doyle's not here by eight-thirty,' ordered Cowley, getting out of the car, 'radio in. Miss Cottingham was anticipating a three-hour tryst.'

'Such stamina, the Latins,' observed Bodie, as his chief made for his own car. 'Must be all that chilli!'

*

Bodie's lightheartedness wouldn't have raised much of a laugh from Frances Cottingham. As Luis approached their room, she was fighting for control. When he opened the door ... when she saw him ... when he held her ... she knew that it would take all her strength and self-control to get through those moments.

She faced the door, her mouth trembling uncontrollably, and when he entered she moved to him quickly, embracing him so that he shouldn't read her expression.

'Frances. *Querida* ...' he said; then was lost in her almost savage hug, feeling the trembling sobs breaking from her body. 'What's the matter? Why are you crying?'

She shook her head: 'It's all right.'

'It doesn't look like it,' he said gently. 'Is it this man who came round ... ?'

'No, no. He was all right.'

'But you said –' he sounded anxious.

'I checked with the Post Office. He was all right.'

'But on the phone last night you seemed so frightened.'

'I'm sorry, it was very silly of me. I get worked up over nothing.'

'But there must have been some reason,' He wanted to be sure.

She improvised: 'It's just ... I'm very on edge. All this secrecy – I hate it.'

'My wife,' he reminded her.

'Your wife's money,' she corrected scathingly.

'That's right.' He didn't argue. 'We've discussed it a dozen times.'

'In this very room!' There was bitterness in her voice, but he seemed not to notice it.

'Among other things,' he agreed; then he smiled, asking her to relax. 'Let's have a drink.' He turned to the attaché case he'd brought with him and took out of it a bottle of Scotch and two glasses. He poured them both a drink, while she watched him – betrayer, betrayed, betrayer ... Suddenly, all she could think of was that she'd never see him again. Never.

'I do love you, Luis,' she said as he handed her the drink.

'Cheers –' and he raised his glass, ignoring – or not hearing – the hurt in her voice.

Not even the rasping of static from an R/T can get through to a man who is singing in his shower: which is why Ray Doyle hadn't answered Bodie's call. Now he stood in the sitting-room of his flat, dressed in a bathrobe, the dirt and dust from the demolished greenhouse sluiced away. The dull thudding on his front door was perfectly audible to him, though. He picked up his gun from the armchair and waited.

'Room service!' Shelley's voice held promise of all sorts of service. Doyle thrust the gun back into its holster and pushed it under the clothes he'd discarded. Then he opened the door to reveal Shelley, stunning in silk shirt and brutally tight jeans, carrying a tray burdened with Bourbon, glasses and a bowl of ice-cubes.

'Hi!' she grinned.

'Hi. When did you get back?' He stood aside to let her in.

'About twenty-five minutes ago. It seemed as good a reason as any to have a drink.'

'Right,' agreed Doyle, grinning. Shelley reached up and touched the congealing line of blood on his chin.

'You okay?'

'There was a guy in your flat,' he told her. 'We had a disagreement.'

'*Another* one?' She almost screeched the question.

'Yeah. Tall, dark, looked like an Arab.'

Shelley simmered down. 'Oh, you mean Carlos. One of our pilots. He uses the place.' She saw his expression and grinned reassuringly '... while I'm away.'

'Nervous sort of guy?' asked Doyle disarmingly.

'Carlos?' She looked puzzled. 'No, a very outgoing sort of guy. Very warm ... very human person.'

'So why did he run away from me?' Doyle queried.

'Did he?'

'Yes.' He waited for an explanation that would ring true.

'Ah, well,' she offered at length, 'he probably thought you were from the bank.'

Doyle looked hurt. 'Do I look as if I'm from the bank?'

'Right now,' laughed Shelley, 'to Carlos everyone looks as if they're from the bank. They're trying to repossess his Porsche. He couldn't keep up the payments.'

Doyle looked as if he was considering the notion. Then – 'He carry a gun, this Carlos?'

'A gun? Heavens, no. He wouldn't hurt a fly.'

'Then it wasn't Carlos,' concluded Doyle neatly. Shelley looked frightened, so he continued. 'Relax. He's gone. And I'm going to get dressed.'

'If you absolutely insist,' she said seductively. Doyle paused; then duty got the better of him and he moved, with great reluctance, towards the bedroom. Shelley smiled. 'I'll open the bar,' she offered. She spent a couple of minutes mixing the drinks, then called: 'Do you want me to dry your back?'

The hell with duty, thought Doyle. 'Now that's what I'd call real Southern hospitality,' he replied.

'One mint-julep,' said Shelley, 'coming up.' She made to go through into the bathroom, then stopped dead. The dull, blued-steel of Doyle's gun was only half-hidden beneath the tangled pile of clothes on the chair. Her face grew hard; the laughter went out of her eyes to be replaced by a cold, ruthless light.

Slowly, she put down the drinks and drew the pistol from its holster.

'Room service! What's keeping you?' Doyle's voice rang out from the bathroom.

Shelley held the gun-barrel up to her cheek for a second. 'Nothing at all ...' she said in a low voice, '... lover!'

A couple of minutes later, when Doyle strolled back into the sitting-room, she had gone. 'Room service in this establishment,' he remarked haughtily, 'is deteriorating rapidly.' Then he noticed that there were two things missing: Shelley – and his gun. He thought for a moment. Then he said: 'Definitely no tip!' A second later he was out of the flat and running, almost bowling over the old witch as she came upstairs. 'She's out; just gone off in a cab,' the woman crowed. Changing direction, Doyle pounded up the stairs to Shelley's flat and without hesitating, began to kick the door down. The old crone watched him reprovingly. 'Temper!' she said mildly.

It took Doyle ten seconds to smash the lock on Shelley's front door and not much longer to check that the place was empty. A minute after that, he was in his car and heading for the rendezvous-point at the hotel.

Frances Cottingham lay in the narrow bed, looking at the scattered clothing on the cheap carpet, and felt ashamed. All passion – all love – had left her; she knew that she'd never feel anything for this man again ... but she hadn't been able to resist him this last time. Even the knowledge that Bodie was listening-in hadn't been enough to kill her desire. But now she shifted in the bed, trying not to touch the man who lay beside her.

Luis sat up and looked at her. 'There is something the matter,' he said.

'Something I ought to tell you,' she replied, watching his face grow wary.

'What is it?'

'That man Khadi I told you about –'

'Oh yes –' the tone was casual, 'what about him?'

'Luis ...' she toyed with the idea of challenging him. 'Why are you so interested in him?'

Outside in the car, Bodie heard and detected the note of rashness in her voice. 'Just tell him the meet, sweetheart,' he muttered. 'Just tell him the meet.'

'I told you,' Luis replied, 'my pieces for *Sabado*.'

'You've never showed them to me.' She still sounded defiant.

'You don't read Spanish.'

'I shouldn't have told you,' she said, still flirting with the truth – the hard truth.

'Don't worry,' he soothed. 'Journalists don't have to reveal their sources. And it all helps to supplement my income. One day I'll have enough so that I won't have to rely on my wife. Then –' The lie came easily to his lips; he smiled; Frances looked at his lying, smiling lips – and it was enough.

'They've changed the meeting-place,' she said abruptly, '– to a hotel. The Crableigh Hotel in Berkshire.'

Bodie breathed a sigh of relief. 'Good girl,' he muttered. Luis' voice came over the earpiece: 'I see. Well, that'll be a nice little scoop for me.' His tone grew seductive as he went on: 'Let's celebrate in advance . . .'

Bodie heard Frances's moan . . . either of passion or disguised distress; either way, he could picture what was happening in that room, behind the net curtains. Grimacing, he switched off the 'bug'. 'Maybe the army would have me back,' he muttered in disgust, and tried to think pure thoughts.

'The Crableigh Hotel' read the ornate sign: 'Private Management.' Cowley and Doad had circled the grounds, checking and double-checking. Eventually, Cowley asked: 'What do you think, Mr Doad?'

The Arab looked satisfied. 'I think I'm unlikely to be disturbed once my guests arrive. If they arrive,' he added cautiously.

'If they do, are you sure you have sufficient men? I can second some of my own people,' Cowley suggested, smiling as he assured Doad: 'They are . . . effective!'

'As I know to my cost,' Doad admitted. 'No: my men have had a lot of experience in dealing with the PMA. We can cope.'

Bodie came in on Cowley's R/T: '3.7. 3.7.'

'Go ahead 3.7.'

'The fish has taken the bait,' Bodie told them. 'Over.'

'Keep playing him,' Cowley ordered. 'He's our big one. Out.'

'To take the bait is one thing,' Doad sounded a note of caution, 'to swallow it quite another.'

'Frances Cottingham has no idea where we are really taking Khadi,' Cowley reminded him, 'even if they realise he's not coming here.'

Doad looked again around the lawns and shrubbery of the quiet country hotel. His eyes narrowed. 'If they do believe her,' he said icily, 'we shall be waiting.'

Doyle was a few streets away from Frances and Luis's hotel, when Bodie's voice crackled through the R/T.

'All right, Doyle, you can stop now. The stud's trophy is yours!' Ray Doyle thought his partner sounded unaccountably edgy. 'Our Latin American contestant has thrown in the towel after an unexpectedly short bout,' continued Bodie acidly. 'Will you now kindly come and look after mum while I escort the gallant loser to his dressing room?'

'Bodie,' said Doyle, pressing the transmit switch, 'I'm very worried about the state of your mind.'

Bodie grinned as he let out the clutch and followed Luis's car away from the hotel. In his rearview mirror, he picked up Doyle, coming slowly into the street and tracking Frances as she set off along the pavement.

Luis had been travelling for some ten minutes before he spotted Bodie: he'd taken a couple of quick turns, to make sure – leaving it to the last minute and not signalling. Bodie stuck; and Luis knew he was being followed. He pulled into the kerb, forcing Bodie to overtake or be obvious. Then he made a fast U-turn. Twenty yards further on, Bodie spun into a handbrake turn, let his momentum spin the wheel back as he straightened, then hit the accelerator hard. At the same time he put out a covering call, giving a description of Luis's car and his general direction. He wove recklessly in and out of the heavy traffic, keeping Luis in sight, but never managing to establish real contact for long – the man was good, using trucks, where he could, to mask his own car so that Bodie wasn't sure whether his quarry might suddenly turn off the road, or attempt to double back.

Finally Bodie managed to get close; but as he manoeuvred to come alongside, Luis swung out from behind the truck he was following, shifted down a gear, and rocketed past.

Bodie wrenched his wheel over to follow and found himself looking down the bonnet of an approaching car. Cursing, he hit the brake, slewing his vehicle off the collision course and completely losing control. The car spun, travelled backwards in a wild, forty-foot skid and stopped, facing the wrong way. Luis was away clear.

'3.7! Where are you?' Cowley's voice cut through on the R/T.

Bodie stopped swearing and looked at it disconsolately. 'I wish I knew!' he said.

Doyle had abandoned his car to follow Frances Cottingham. She'd taken a foot-bridge at the end of a cul-de-sac that brought her out into a main thoroughfare. Doyle didn't think she was trying to lose him – didn't think she knew he was there – but he was taking no chances. He watched her as she paused at the kerbside; her eyes were troubled, her face tight with tension and distress. Doyle couldn't be sure, but she seemed to be mumbling something to herself ... her lips working crookedly as she stood by the busy road.

What happened next took Doyle completely by surprise. Looking neither left nor right, she stepped off the kerb straight into the path of an approaching car. Her body flew into the air, slammed into the bonnet of the car that had struck her, then crashed into the road in a flurry of twisted limbs. Then she lay still.

Doyle raced across the street and knelt to cradle her head. His other hand grasped the butt of his pistol as the driver of the car came sprinting back. The man looked at the gun, then at Doyle. 'No!' he pleaded. 'I didn't have a chance. She stepped right out in front of me!' He was plainly terrified – terrified and shocked. Doyle holstered the gun. 'Let's get her to hospital. Fast!' he urged. The motorist continued to stare at the agent, transfixed by having seen the pistol. Doyle yelled an order: 'Come on!' Gently, he began to lift Frances Cottingham out of the road.

Several hours later, Doyle walked into the briefing room at CI5's Whitehall HQ. Like the building itself, the room was unexceptional – functional. No flags, no plaques, no plush furnishings. Nothing to show that the toughest branch of British Intelligence operated there. Cowley and Bodie were waiting for him.

'Well?' Cowley was deliberately businesslike.

'Dead on arrival,' said Doyle; his voice betrayed no trace of emotion.

'And the American girl?'

'Not a dickey bird,' Doyle told him. 'Vanished.'

'Obviously not too impressed with English men,' cut in Bodie.

Doyle wasn't in the mood for humour. He shot his partner a sour look and said: 'No more so than the Latin lover with English driving, from what I hear.'

Cowley sounded impatient with the pair of them. 'Do you mind,' he snapped, 'if we save the post-mortems till after Khadi's left the country? In one piece!'

Doyle turned to the matter in hand: 'When does he arrive?'

'Ten tomorrow morning,' Cowley said.

Bodie looked at his watch. 'Great,' he said sarcastically. 'Should get all of three hours sleep.'

'I doubt it,' Cowley said, unapologetically. 'I want you

there by seven. Take Jameson and a couple of others. Stake out the perimeter.'

Doyle looked at him balefully. 'Am I in the doghouse, or what?'

'If you are,' suggested Bodie, 'take your bloody R/T with you this time.'

Cowley ignored the banter. 'You're in the Crableigh Hotel,' he told Doyle. 'I want someone to keep an eye on Doad. See he doesn't go over the top.'

'They won't try and hit him at the airfield,' observed Bodie moodily, 'it's too open. They'll go for him at Crableigh. It's *me* who's in the doghouse.' He flashed a look at Cowley – plainly asking to be the one with a real chance of action.

'You will be if you persist in questioning my orders, Bodie.' Cowley's tone was pure steel. 'We know that Frances told him the meet had been changed but we don't know if he believed her. If he didn't, they may decide to hit Khadi at the airfield.' The men looked at each other. They'd laid a trap. It remained to be seen just how clever the prey really was!

Chapter Fifteen

The Lear jet emerged through the cloud cover, made a single, exploratory pass over the small airfield, then set down in a perfect three-point landing. Bodie watched it taxi to a halt, then switched his gaze to the large black limousine and the figures of Cowley, Masterson and Alousha standing nearby. He waited until he could see Khadi leaving the plane, with the reception committee moving towards him, then he signalled his men along the perimeter to move in, slowly, tightening the defensive circle.

Khadi and Alousha embraced, Alousha wincing slightly as Khadi's hand clapped him affectionately in the small of the back. Then Masterson stepped forward to shake hands and to introduce Cowley. The party began to walk towards the limo; Bodie and the other CI5 agents closed in, still watching for signs of trouble.

As Khadi reached the car, he caught sight of Alousha's grimace and remembered the wince as they'd embraced. 'You don't seem very well, Abdul.' He was concerned.

Alousha made a moue. 'A case of British tummy, I fear, sir.'

'I'm sorry to hear that,' commiserated Cowley, helping Alousha into the car.

Khadi looked round. 'Where's Doad?' he wanted to know.

Cowley smiled reassuringly. 'He's supervising security elsewhere sir.'

The limo's doors closed with an expensive *thunk* and the car moved off. Close behind, Bodie and two CI5 men rested Uzzi submachine guns across their knees, never taking their eyes off the lead car for a second.

The black limo that swept into the drive of the Crableigh Hotel was being watched just as closely: by Doad and four of his men. They were hoping – praying – that their enemy would take the bait. The car came to a stop by the front door of the hotel and a figure – Khadi's stand-in for the operation – leapt out and hurried towards the building, covered by Doad and the chauffeur. He reached the portal and disappeared into the hotel. Doad lifted his R/T: 'They didn't believe her, Doyle.' He looked bitterly disappointed.

In a thick stand of trees some sixty yards from the house, Doyle was standing over a surprised Luis Delgado, his gun-muzzle almost touching the man's temple. He snapped down the switch on his R/T. 'Oh, but they did, Doad,' he replied. 'They did.'

Doad and the rest of his men arrived within seconds, one of them snatching the loaded haversack Delgado was carrying and sorting through it, while another frisked the man himself.

Doad rested his pistol against Luis's chest. 'Who are you?' he asked harshly. 'Tell me!'

Doyle reached inside Luis's pocket and located his wallet – at about the same moment as Doad's man emptied the contents of the haversack out on to the grass. There were cameras, a slim rifle-mike and tape-recorder, night lenses . . . no explosives; no guns.

Luis chose this moment to speak: 'As far as I know it's not against the law to take photographs. Not against English law, anyway.'

Doad was confused. 'I don't give a damn about English law,' he spat angrily.

'Well, it's what we're enforcing around here, as of now,' Doyle butted in.

Doad was furious. 'I had an agreement with Cowley –' he began.

'Your agreement with Cowley covered the treatment of Arab terrorists,' Doyle cautioned, 'so I suggest you all put your safety catches back on.' He handed Doad a card that he'd taken from the wallet. It read: 'Simon

Jacob Bloom, Cultural Attaché, Embassy of Israel, 2, Palace Gdn. W.8.'

Doad looked at it, astonished. 'Israeli Intelligence!' he managed at last.

The prisoner looked at him, amused. 'An Israeli cultural attaché, interested in English country houses,' he said.

'You can wipe that grin off your face,' Doyle told him. 'I'm nicking you for trespassing.' At about that point, it occurred to Ray Doyle to wonder where the real action might be taking place.

Alousha leaned forward, clutching his stomach, his face screwed up with pain. Khadi patted him comfortingly, and spoke a couple of words to Masterson who tapped Cowley on the shoulder. 'Our friend feels sick,' he shrugged, looking to Cowley for guidance.

'Can't you hang on for five minutes?' asked Cowley. 'It's just up the road.' Alousha shook his head; he seemed to be losing the battle for control.

Bodie was aware of something happening in the car in front, but couldn't make out what it was. He tried to identify the various passengers; then his attention was taken by a Land Rover parked at an intersection, its bonnet up and a young girl, her back to Bodie, bending over the engine. The image flashed on his brain, registering for only a second before he noticed the lead car coming to a halt.

'What's going on?' he rasped into the R/T.

'Mr Alousha,' came Cowley's reply. 'He's got a problem.' Alousha left the limo at a run, bent double and clutching his stomach, and made for the roadside trees. Bodie watched; something was happening; he felt it – something wrong; but he couldn't pin it down. When he glanced in the rear-view mirror, he noticed that the Land-Rover had disappeared. Bodie's memory was working frantically ... something he'd seen ... something he'd recognised. Then, in an explosive flash of understanding, it came to him. A girl, bending over the engine: one leg raised, the denim stretched tightly, flower-patches sewn on to the back-pocket!

'The American girl! Shelley Hunter!' he rapped into the R/T. 'That was her in that Land-Rover.'

Cowley didn't hesitate. 'Go!' he roared at the chauffeur. 'Go on! *Drive on!*'

The man hesitated as Masterson asked. 'What about Alousha?'

Cowley drove his pistol into the chauffeur's ribs: no time now for niceties. 'Drive!' he ordered. The car sped away leaving broad wheel-scars on the soft verge.

From the fringe of trees came a sudden whooshing roar as a wire guided rocket hurtled towards the road, crossing the space where the car had stood and erupting in an inferno of billowing flame in a facing spinney. Shelley, who had picked up Alousha, was driving the Land-Rover hard towards the rocket-launcher. Another missile swooped after the limo, missing it by no more than a few feet, as Bodie and the two other CI5 men rushed the position, their submachine guns flaying the brush with a murderous fan-tail of lead. When their clips emptied, they still ran straight for the launcher, throwing their machine-guns aside and drawing hand-guns.

The man who had been firing the missiles emerged from cover, staggering. Another bullet took him full in the throat and he flopped back, gargling in his own blood. Shelley changed direction, ploughing through the undergrowth and coming at the CI5 agents head-on. Bodie stood his ground, calmly lining the Land-Rover up in his sights and emptying his gun.

He watched the windscreen star and shatter, watched as water spurted from the radiator, watched as the headlight disintegrated. Still the Land-Rover bore down on him. Then, as if some great hand had slammed into it, the vehicle careered sideways and smashed into a clump of trees.

Bodie raced over, thumping another clip into his automatic. He needn't have bothered. Alousha and Shelley were too shaken to offer any resistance ... except that Shelley managed, 'You bastard!'

Doyle looked at her pitilessly. 'Just like a woman,' he said. He turned to one of the back-up team who had arrived at his elbow. 'Would you believe it,' he asked, not taking his eyes from Shelley and Alousha for a minute, 'if I told you that less than a week ago this same lady was telling me that she thought British policemen were wonderful.'

'Murderers!' Shelley's eyes filled with hate.

'No,' said the agent, answering Bodie's question. The big A-squad man smiled mirthlessly. 'Didn't think you would,' he said; and met Shelley's loathing with his own, level, remorseless look.